THE DUKE OF DISORDER

The Rakes of Mayhem
Book 3

Anna St. Claire

ARE YOU SIGNED UP FOR DRAGONBLADE'S BLOG?

You'll get the latest news and information on exclusive giveaways, exclusive excerpts, coming releases, sales, free books, cover reveals and more.

Check out our complete list of authors, too!

No spam, no junk. That's a promise!

Sign Up Here

www.dragonbladepublishing.com

Dearest Reader;

Thank you for your support of a small press. At Dragonblade Publishing, we strive to bring you the highest quality Historical Romance from some of the best authors in the business. Without your support, there is no 'us', so we sincerely hope you adore these stories and find some new favorite authors along the way.

Happy Reading!

CEO, Dragonblade Publishing

Additional Dragonblade books by Author Anna St. Claire

The Rakes of Mayhem Series
The Earl of Excess (Book 1)
The Marquess of Mischief (Book 2)
The Duke of Disorder (Book 3)

The Lyon's Den Connected World
Lyon's Prey

PROLOGUE

Richmond, Surrey, England
January 1813

"NICHOLS, WHAT DO you mean, she is *not available to me?*" demanded Lucas Pemberton, the Marquess of Somers.

He could not imagine this being her idea of a joke. Only a sennight ago, he and Harriett had spoken of their feelings for each other and planned to marry. While they had not been formally betrothed, he planned to take care of that detail. Her father was in London handing some business affairs, and Lucas had planned to ask for his permission upon her father's return. Richmond sat just outside of London, and he expected her father back at any time. After courting for months, Lucas had finally gathered enough courage to ask her father for her hand. *He loved her.* They had planned a picnic for today. He had sent a missive two days ago, reminding her of his return and the picnic. And saying he could not wait to hold her in his arms, again.

The tall, graying butler peered down at him. "My lord," he said with a strained voice. "She is *married.*"

The words knocked him backwards. Lucas felt as if he had been punched in the stomach. He swallowed and took a calming breath. "Is *his lordship* available to me?" he persisted, balling his fists at his side, refusing to believe that Harriett would intentionally make a fool of him. There had been no word from her. What had happened to the missive? Something seemed very wrong here.

After a long pause, the butler answered. "My lord, Lord Scarsdale has given me strict instructions . . ."

"Please request he see me," Lucas said, cutting him off.

"Very well." Nichols moved to close the door, but Lucas stopped it from closing.

"I will wait here," Lucas said quietly but firmly.

The man nodded and left the door partially open. A few minutes later, he returned. "My lord, Lord Scarsdale will see you. Please follow me."

Lucas had been in this house many times, but never had he felt so unwelcome. His footfalls on the dark, tiled granite echoed, and the dark paneling of the hall gave an ominous sense. Nichols opened the door and announced him. Lucas schooled himself to be calm. There had to be an explanation.

"Lord Somers. Have a seat," Scarsdale pointed to the leather seat in front of his desk.

Lucas noticed the man staggered slightly and gripped his chair for support, sitting down and leaning over the desk. "I left a message for you, yet you insisted on seeing me, as if that could change things," the earl puffed.

"I do not understand. What has happened?" Lucas said, fighting queasiness. The man had done something to his daughter—his *Harriett*. "Where is she?"

"Gone. She is married. She is Lady Dudley, now," he said, not meeting his eyes.

Lucas stood and leaned over the desk. "What do you mean, she is Lady Dudley? Your daughter and I have been courting for months. I asked your permission to court her. Remember?" he said, gripping the side of the desk to avoid gripping the man's collar. Understanding dawned on him. "You married your daughter to Lord Dudley? *What have you done?*"

The man paled and leaned back in his chair. "It is no business of yours. She is married. Harriett is a good daughter, and she will live a good life. Maybe not the life she wanted, but she is my child, and it was my right to decide these things . . ."

"I was coming to ask you for her hand. You knew this—I had sent word that I needed to speak with you concerning Harriett. *Where is she?*" Lucas roared, straining not to pummel the man.

Her father hung his head.

Hurried footfalls sounded behind him. "Lord Somers, you are too late. My husband made his daughter marry to repay some sort of *obligation*," the countess spat from behind him. "Good luck receiving any details. Not even I know how this came to pass."

Lucas looked from the countess to her husband and narrowed his gaze. "If you needed money, you could have come to me or to my father."

"My daughter pleaded, and I tried to stop it, your lordship." Lady Scarsdale shot a disgusted look at her husband. "There is nothing that can be done, Lord Somers. Harriett did her duty by her father. She is a married woman, now," Lady Scarsdale said, acidly.

"You do not understand. I had to," Lord Scarsdale said, listing slightly as he poured himself a drink.

"When?" Lucas demanded.

"P . . . pardon?" the earl stammered, unsteadily, swishing a small amount of amber liquid from the top of the glass.

"*When?* When did she marry?" Lucas insisted, his voice louder.

"Two days ago," her father said, setting his emptied glass on his desk. "Do you think I wanted to do this? You are a marquess. What father would not have wanted his daughter to ultimately be a duchess? There was nothing I could do. You must try to understand."

Understand? He understood that his head throbbed and the woman he had planned to marry—*the woman he loved*—had been forced to marry another. *This must be a bad dream.* How could a father have done this to his daughter? "You sold your daughter into a life she could not have wanted, as if she was a dog you discarded," he seethed, his voice low and steady.

"Now see here!" the earl said, walking up to him.

"*You* see here!" Blinded with rage, Lucas grabbed him with his left arm and pulled back his right fist, intent on smashing the callous man in the face. Instead, he let the earl go and backed up. The older man staggered from drink and fell to the floor. Lucas stepped back, turned, and strode from the room. Her father was right. *There was nothing he could do if Harriett was married to another.* If she had married Dudley, he doubted he would ever hear from her again.

CHAPTER ONE

Richmond, Surrey, London
January 1818

"*G*OD'S TEETH! WHO the hell placed me in the betting book . . . *with a bet of marriage?*" roared Lucas Pemberton, the fourth Duke of Dorman, closely eyeing the penmanship of the entry. "Of all things! Fess up! It looks like your handwriting," he said, before slamming the book shut and turning to his friend, Evan Prescott, the Earl of Clarendon.

The man laughed uproariously. "I deny any recollection of doing such a thing."

Lucas narrowed his eyes at his friend. "You deny *recollection?* If I recall, a bet got *you* married, and you denied that, until you could not," Dorman said, in good humor.

"You cannot remain unmarried. You are the only one not leg-shackled among us," Romney quipped. "Once there was a bet amongst us on who would be the last, and with Banbury recently wed, we lost that. It appears we fail at bets!" The Earl of Romney slapped his friend Clarendon on the back. "Was it you?"

"No. I swear!" the Earl of Clarendon answered in denial. "I would never have done such a thing."

"That does not answer who placed me in the book, although it makes me suspect you, Clarendon," returned Lucas, in good-natured tones. "Seriously, which one of you rakes did it?"

"Ahem. We are no longer rakes . . . except perhaps for you," drawled Clarendon.

"Perhaps someone has targeted you . . . the father of an aging spinster, perhaps? Or maybe a brother wishing to retire his responsibilities for shepherding his marriageable sister on the market. As an older brother, that is understandable. Who would have thought marriage would agree with any of us, when we swore all those years ago to remain single?" offered Romney, in a helpful tone. "A minor bet should be of no consequence."

"How long do you plan to keep your bachelorhood, Dorman?" the Earl of Clarendon teased, leaning back in their club's russet brown leather chair, and sipping his brandy. "I would never have willingly become leg-shackled, but I rather enjoy it."

"Yes, and we all adore your Charlotte. But marriage is not for me," Lucas Pemberton, the fourth Duke of Dorman, replied. "I will not be marrying. Perhaps I felt it was right for me at one time, but Providence intervened and set me right."

"That was a long time ago and deuced unfortunate," Clarendon returned. "And I doubt Providence means for you to be an aging old man without a wife or children."

Four boys had sworn an oath of brotherhood while attending Eton years ago and had blazed quite a reputation across London as rakes. Today, three had found love and married. Only Lucas remained single. As the fourth Duke of Dorman, he was expected to marry and produce an heir, but marriage was the last thing on his mind. Only one woman had come close to ensnaring him years ago. Lucas performed his duties as duke—including hosting balls for his mother at their London home and their country estate in Sussex—but he cut a wide berth around the marriage-minded women and their mamas. "Ha! A minor bet got *you* hitched if I recall correctly, Clarendon," laughed Dorman.

"It was not me," Clarendon persisted.

"So, you say," teased Romney, good naturedly, as they left Dorman's club and crossed the street where their horses were stabled.

Each man paid the young stablehand and mounted his horse, beginning the ride to Pembley Manor, Dorman's country estate.

"With Banbury married, I feel like a fifth wheel. It is rather nice that you and your wives accepted my invitation to spend time at Pembley Manor," Lucas admitted. Their friend, Christopher Anglesey, the Marquess of Banbury, had married Lady Diana Lawrence on Christmas Eve in London. Following Banbury's nuptials, Clarendon, Romney, and their wives had taken a side trip to the Dorman estate and were spending time together before heading home, while the marquess and marchioness left for their honeymoon.

"Gabe, was Smitty able to change his shoes?" Lucas said as he met the ostler and prepared to mount.

"Aye, Your Grace," the young ostler returned, holding the reins of the duke's steed.

"Please help me!" A female voice screamed as a black horse flew past, cutting across the street and into the alleyway behind the mews.

Lucas Pemberton grabbed the reins back and hoisted himself into the saddle. "Come on, Dirk," he urged his horse, gaining speed on the woman. He saw the horse cross High Street, as horse and rider tore through the mews, as people scattered to escape being run over. Street peddlers pushed and shoved their carts to move out of her way as her horse turned onto Richmond Road.

As he got close, he realized the woman's booted foot was caught in the stirrup, twisted, as she held to the horn of the saddle. She appeared to be struggling to release her foot from the boot. He was almost upon her when a coach and four ripped around the corner, heading straight at them. Without a moment to spare, Dirk pulled alongside. "Hold on," Lucas coaxed as he grabbed her horse's reins.

"I *am* . . . holding. Please make her stop," the woman pleaded.

"Whoa boy . . ."

He tugged gently on Dirk's reins, while pulling the spooked horse's reins firmly, effectively slowing both horses to a trot.

As soon as Dirk stopped, he slid down and grabbed the woman by the shoulders. She shook violently as he released her boot from the stirrup. She tested her foot and as she stood, she lost her balance, falling into him.

"I apologize, my lord," she said, offering a smile before looking into his face and returning his look of shock.

"Lady Dudley," Lucas said, stiffening as realization hit.

An icy chill shot through him. Clarendon and Romney rode up behind them but stood quietly on their mounts about twenty yards behind. He felt certain they recognized the lady as well. Her father's abrupt dismissal of their courtship and informal betrothal, and her subsequent marriage to another almost five years ago, had broken his heart. Her father had used her to pay off some sort of debt. However, Lucas had never been able to find out anything about its nature. He assumed it had been a gambling debt, but the man never said.

Having lost the woman he loved, Lucas had not mentioned her name in years. He had finally stopped thinking of her every time he spotted a woman with blonde hair that resembled her. He hated the soirees and balls he was forced to attend, and had vowed to never lose his heart again.

At one time, all four of the boys . . . now men . . . had pledged to avoid matrimony—at least until they had sown what their parents referred to as their *wild oats*. Banbury's marriage made Lucas the last bachelor.

"Y . . . Your Grace," Lady Harriett Dudley stammered, her face heating with color. "What are you doing here?"

"I live here, if you recall," he said tersely, catching himself staring into her green eyes. *You are the one that no longer lives here.* "Your ankle . . . are you able to stand on it?" Lucas asked, this time in a much softer tone, realizing he still held her close, while others were watching.

Wordlessly, she nodded.

Her hair smelled like roses. It had *always* smelled of roses—
the scent triggered memories of the last time he had held her.
Lucas had heard nothing from her in the five years since the night
he had promised to see her father and ask his permission to marry
her. He had finally accepted the loss from his life but had never
understood what had happened. Even his father had inquired into
the matter. Still, her father had refused to say anything, leaving
him forced to deal with the simple truth that Harriett was
married. It left him with unanswered questions and a broken
heart. Inwardly, he cursed himself for not allowing Clarendon or
Romney to rescue the woman. But he had reacted out of concern.

Raw emotion surged and threatened to throw him off-
kilter—the same emotions that lurked even today and barely
stayed walled away from his heart. He released her and stepped
back. "This is a . . . surprise." His tone was stiff. A year ago, word
had reached him that Dudley had died following a riding
accident. Lucas had not reached out to her—feeling she knew
where to find him—if she needed him. She had not reached out,
and even while he understood the strict social mores of mourning, it still galled him there had been no word. Finally, he had
accepted she was gone from his life.

To see her here today shocked his senses.

She had not moved from where he had deposited her and had
maintained her gaze upon his face. Lucas thought he read
disbelief in her eyes. "Perhaps you should test it," he said,
indicating her ankle, and eager to divert her arresting eyes.

"Oh . . . oh, yes," she said finally. Without a word, she
reached out and gripped his arm for security as she tested her
ankle. Pain paled her face. "I believe I have injured it, Your
Grace." As if she had just realized she had used his arm for
support, she withdrew her arm and thrust it into the folds of her
lavender dress.

"May I?" he asked, crouching down to look at her ankle.

She nodded, nibbling nervously on her lower lip.

Lucas lifted the bottom of her dress to reveal her ankle. He gently lifted it and could see the first signs of swelling and bruising appear. He tested the skin and felt a familiar pang of longing shoot through him. *Damn and blast it,* he thought. How could it be possible she still roused the same effect in him these many years later? "It appears to be twisted, or perhaps sprained, from being caught in the stirrup," he said softly, still holding her ankle. "I should see you home. I assume you are staying with your parents?" he asked. Their manor house was several miles away. He signaled to his friends, who still sat waiting, and they slowly moved in his direction.

"I suppose it would be foolhardy to ride with my ankle swelling. However, I do not wish to inconvenience Your Grace," she offered, attempting mundane conversation.

"Nonsense!" Clarendon said cheerfully, riding up in time to hear her. "Lady Dudley. It is a pleasure to meet you, finally." He nodded politely. "And this is Lord Matthew Romney. The three of us are all headed in that direction. You can ride with His Grace, and we will bring your horse along behind."

Lucas shot Clarendon a look of irritation. The last thing he needed was to ride with her against his chest for several miles.

"Yes!" Romney added. "We are glad to be of assistance. We are headed back to the manor to check on our wives before they search for us," he said with a laugh.

"If it will not be too much trouble," she finally answered in a hurt voice. "I am visiting my parents."

"For how long?" Romney asked.

Lucas noticed his friends were prattling on, as if she was a long-lost friend of theirs, ignoring his obvious discomfort. He gave a forced smile and nod before mounting his horse. Romney handed her up to him with a knowing smile and shot him a wink. He scowled back, but Harriett shifted in the seat before finally settling against him. *I am in trouble.*

HARRIETT COULD NOT believe she was sitting in front of Lucas Pemberton. On his horse, no less. She fought the impulse to snuggle against him and close her eyes, but was too aware of the eyes upon her, as well as his reaction to her presence. His friends stayed silent and rode behind them. She would have thought to feel their condemnation, but they had been extremely gracious and helpful—everyone except Lucas, who appeared to want little to do with her.

The last person she had expected to run into was her former *almost* betrothed. She had placed the "almost" in there only to help rationalize why she had not reached back out to him—*ever*. Of course, she could not while her husband lived. He closeted her off from all her family and her friends—anyone connected with her past. She had written to Lucas a few times, but when she never received word from him, she had stopped.

When Dudley died, she still had not reached out. She had kept up with him, and knew he had not married, but with certainty, she knew he was not waiting for her. What would have been the use of that? Her father had broken his heart. *She* had broken his heart. His father had been a duke, and she was certain he would have tried to help his son. The older duke had died a few years ago, making Lucas the new duke. She tried to reach out then, fearing her husband's reaction if he found out. She had wondered if the three missives she had written to Lucas that first year had made it to him.

That mystery was solved when Dudley died and she found them in his things, bundled up tightly, obviously read and reread many times. It would explain some of the bruising blows he occasionally delivered her way. The servants had been his spies, and she learned that early on and trusted no one.

Harriett should have reached out for help *and wanted to*. She penned missives many times to her family, only to crumble and toss them into the fire. Without understanding *why* her always kind father had made her marry Dudley to satisfy some sort of debt, she could not. The thought always made her stop, unsure of what had happened and afraid her actions would harm her family.

The minute she saw him, she knew.

Her heart still belonged to Lucas.

It mattered not. She would never marry again. Harriett would never willingly place herself under the control of a man again—*ever!* An icy shiver ran down her spine. Dudley had been dead a little over a year, but the memories of their union ran fresh in her mind.

Lucas had said nary a word. His presence was stiff, unyielding. Closing her eyes tightly, she settled herself against his chest, allowing herself to focus on him—the smell of his bergamot cologne, a smell she had missed for five years, the warmth of his chest, and the beating of his heart. She had longed for this man. She wished she had done some things differently—perhaps, had she only demanded answers instead of meekly obeying her father. Maybe then she would not be the widow of a man she detested— but at least she was his widow, and no longer his wife. Instead, she might have children and look forward to her days. Yet, even as she thought it, she knew it had been impossible. She could never have spoken so to her father thus, and she had been but ten and eight.

"You seem very quiet. Does your ankle pain you?" he asked.

His voice broke in on her thoughts and she stared into his deep brown eyes, struggling to recall his words. "It throbs, but it is not too painful. Could it be broken?" she asked.

In response, Lucas squeezed her shoulder with his free hand. Shock overtook his expression as he seemed to realize what he had done.

"I . . . was too familiar. I apologize. It is a habit I would have thought had disappeared with time," he said in a strained voice.

"Your Grace. It is *I* who should apologize. I must have appeared out of nowhere for you." She took a fortifying glance away before again looking into his eyes. "There is nothing I can say to make it seem better between us, and this . . ." she pointed to her ankle, "Makes things even more awkward. I have placed you in this impossible position, even though it was never my intention."

"Lady Dudley, all that you say is true. I regret my contribution to your discomfiture," he said hoarsely. "I never meant that to be. However, you *are* the last person I expected to see today—or ever again."

She gulped. His tone sounded so matter of fact. Harriett glanced around and noticed they were approaching her parents' manor.

"I still have a question, if I may ask," he said.

Surprised, she raised her gaze. "What is that, Your Grace?"

"In this moment alone, away from anyone hearing us, I must ask it. Why . . . why did you never contact me?" he asked, his eyes holding her gaze.

"I . . . I wanted to. I tried. But my f . . . father...," she stammered, trying to answer him. Harriett straightened. "The arrangement was beyond my control. My father took me away to marry. Dudley was there with a license, and I had no choice. Why . . . I never knew. All he said was, he was sorry."

Lucas's face reddened. "My father tried to intervene, but nothing could be done."

She looked away. She would have wanted nothing more than to be in his arms these past five years. Awareness washed over her. There was no going back . . . not after what had passed between them. They had forced her to marry another. At eighteen years, she could not refuse her father's wish that she marry Dudley. She quaked at the thought. Even now, her husband's reach seemed beyond the grave. "Your father could not have stopped it. My father had already agreed."

"*Why?* Losing you nearly destroyed me. Your father had blessed our courtship. Nothing made sense."

"Lucas . . . Your Grace . . . I do not know." She drew a shaky breath, determined not to cry. "You would have to ask him. He has never told me, despite my pleading. I doubt you will get an answer." She swallowed. "I wrote you, but the staff . . . they gave my letters to Dudley, who punished me for writing them, although I did not realize that had been his impetus until he died, and I found my unsent letters. By then, too much time had passed."

Her family's large, pink-stoned manor stood in front of her. Canton Manor had been *home* for most of her life, except for the five years she had lived as Dudley's wife in Kent. "They are in London, right now," she offered, as two footmen came down the steps to assist her. "I had planned to leave when they returned, but this may keep me here a little longer," she said, looking at her ankle.

"She has injured her ankle," Lucas said, abruptly handing her down to the care of a footman who had scurried down the front steps at their arrival.

"Yes, Your Grace," the footman replied.

"Timmons, I wish to walk," Harriett spoke up.

"It would be better if you would allow someone to carry you," Lucas whispered.

Timmons lowered her to the ground and steadied her as the other footman headed toward her horse.

"I will take her to the stable, my lord," the footman said to Clarendon, accepting the reins of Harriett's horse.

"Allow me to assist," Lucas said, sliding down from his horse.

"I will be fine . . ." Harriett started.

"Nonsense. You will allow me to take you inside to the parlor, and I will have a doctor summoned. It is the least I can do."

Timmons nodded and stepped aside. Lucas picked her up and hurried ahead of the footman.

"Good afternoon, Your Grace," the butler said with a bewildered look on his face.

"Nichols, summon the doctor. I will place her in the parlor," Lucas said decisively. "A mishap with the stirrups happened and her foot got caught. I managed to stop her mount."

"Yes, Your Grace. I will see to the doctor right away." The butler tugged a brown bell pull inside the parlor, then left them alone.

Lucas glanced down at Harriett, whose arms were wrapped about his neck. His face hovered very close to hers. Softly parted lips and green eyes gazing into his tempted him, as his heart and his desires warred with each other. The lure of the moment nearly made him falter. "I will leave you in your family's capable hands," he said with a weary look on his face. Her hands slid from his shoulders as he placed her on the parlor sofa. He turned to leave, but stopped and faced her.

"Thank you, Luc . . . Your Grace," she murmured, correcting herself.

"We are alone and can still be friends. You may still call me Lucas," he said softly. "I will leave you now." He glanced her way once more before closing the door. "It was good to see you, Harriett." With those words, he left.

CHAPTER TWO

T HE THREE MEN rode in companionable silence toward Pembley Manor, the Dorman estate, where they planned to adjourn to Lucas' game room for billiards and cigars.

Once arriving at the entrance, they handed the horses to the awaiting groom.

It was Clarendon who finally broke the silence. "Do you want to talk about it?" he asked, walking to the corner cabinet and extracting the glasses. Taking off the stopper, he poured brandy into each of the glasses.

"I am not sure what there is to say," Lucas said, finally.

"That is all? Did she provide any clue to what happened?" Romney asked, extracting a cue stick and examining the tip.

"No. I asked. She still knows no reason her father married her to Lord Dudley," Lucas said. He shook his head, as if to clear it. "I feel as confused as I did the last time I stood at the door to her father's house."

Clarendon passed out the glasses and pulled a cue stick from the rack. Romney racked the balls and Lucas set the cue ball opposite the triangle of balls.

"I believe the last time we played, it ended on your turn to break," Lucas said, nodding to Clarendon. "Romney, you play this one. I will play the winner."

Clarendon nodded and set his drink on the side of the table.

CRACK. The balls scattered with a red one hitting the side pocket, followed by the cue ball. "I scratched," he said, shaking his head. He dug out the ball and placed it in the lower center of the table.

The sound of balls hitting each other and bouncing off the felt-covered cushioned rails continued in silence for twenty minutes.

"That's game!" Romney said, cheerfully, sipping his drink.

The men shifted and Lucas took his place, prepared to break the balls, when his mother sailed into the room. "Darling, you have received a post by special messenger," she said, smiling as she walked up to her son, handing him the missive, and bussing a kiss on his cheek.

"Mother! I wondered if you were back from shopping," Lucas said, returning her kiss and breaking the seal on the note. "Did the ladies enjoy the trip into Richmond?"

"We had a good time and spent most of our time perusing some new patterns." The duchess quirked a brow as she looked from one to the other of the men. "You are all rather quiet up here. This game feels serious," she teased.

"And you are a welcomed diversion, Mother," Lucas said with a grin and squeezed her shoulder affectionately. Taking his hand away, he was reminded of the same gesture he made with Harriett. She had not changed.

"I am glad to help where I can," she said with a smile. "I ordered a plate of food for you boys. Rawlings should bring it in a few minutes."

"This might be a good time for a break. Would you like a glass of sherry, Mother?" Lucas asked, walking to the cabinet.

"No, darling. I will wait until dinner. I just wanted to say hello. It is so nice to see the three of you together. If Lord Banbury was here, it would be like old times with the four of you!"

The missive was burning a hole in his hand. It must have seemed important for Mother to bring it straight to them.

Lucas took a moment to read the letter. He closed his eyes

and looked up at the ceiling as if imploring Divine Providence to intercede on his behalf.

"Well, what was it? The messenger told Egerton it was extremely important that you see it as quickly as possible," his mother prodded.

When Lucas failed to give an immediate response, Clarendon put down his glass and walked to the rack of billiard sticks hanging on the wall, prepared to return his. "Perhaps we should leave you two alone if . . ."

"No. No, it is quite all right," Lucas interjected, cutting him off. "It is a brief note from a solicitor. I am sure whatever it says, I can handle it later." Yet, he continued to read, unable to believe what he was reading.

Finally, looking up in disbelief, he took a deep breath. "The post informs me I am to be the guardian for two young ladies, ages twelve and sixteen." He glanced up before continuing. "A distant cousin and his wife died of influenza while their two girls were away at school. Albert asked me *years* ago if I would serve as guardian. It was one of those things you agree to in that moment, but never give a thought to it coming to pass. It is an awful tragedy for the girls to lose their parents. I gave my consent and will honor it. Mother, we shall have two young ladies to shepherd into Society." Lucas ran his hands through his hair in frustration. "I do not recall ever meeting the girls."

"Oh, my! I had not received word that Albert and his wife had succumbed. I only this week received a post that his lovely wife, Edwina, had been feeling poorly. How positively wretched for those girls. I must send a return note to the family. Does it say when the funeral will be?" the dowager duchess asked.

Once he had a moment to digest it all, he realized his mother appropriately brushed past his frustration and focused on the loss of his family. "It appears they held it two weeks past. Their solicitor penned the missive. Mr. Surety writes that the girls will arrive by hired coach within a day or so," he muttered.

"That could be any day now. Please tell me the man has not

sent those young girls unescorted!" his mother said, alarmed.

"No. I see an aunt volunteered to accompany them, but he added that she indicated she must return immediately afterward," Lucas replied. "A Miss Esther Stewart. The note mentions she is Albert's father's spinster sister. We should prepare a room for them," he murmured distractedly, attempting to absorb this news.

"I wonder why we were not informed?" his mother asked, apparently still concerned about the funeral, and possibly affronted by the omission.

"Mother," he said, softening his voice. "I will inquire how we may be of help to the family. For now, it seems we need to ready the house for two young ladies." He wiped his brow and gulped down his drink. Quietly, he regarded Romney, who appeared to be struggling against smiling. "Watch it!" he mouthed to his friend, good-naturedly.

"I cannot imagine your meaning, my friend," Romney replied in a serious tone. "How can we help? My wife is in Town and will be glad to assist, although she is not schooled in many of the disciplines the young lady of England needs to know—the pianoforte, painting and the like. Although, she knows French, and herbal medicine." He paused. "Had she not known the medicine, I may not have survived to be here today."

"A worthy knowledge, to be sure. Lady Romney has many wonderful attributes," Lucas said.

"I shall do my best to assist you, Son," his mother chimed in, clearly distracted.

"I appreciate that, Mother. As I only have brothers, I do not know what to expect with young ladies," Lucas said, giving a heavenward glance. His two younger brothers were away at school at the moment.

"From my experience growing up with a sister, they can be quite fun to have around. Charlotte always kept our household lively," Romney offered.

"Perhaps you need to consider a governess," Clarendon said

with a look that reminded Lucas of a cat that swallowed the canary. "*And a wife*," his friend added, purposely coughing the words so Lucas barely heard them.

He recognized Clarendon's teasing and ignored it. "I agree. That is a good thought, Mother. We will appreciate any help and guidance you can give me," he said, in almost a pleading voice.

"Yes, dear," she replied, still sounding distracted. "If you can excuse me, I will alert the cook and Mrs. Blaine to the arrivals and request some sustenance readied and have the rooms prepared, as well as the nursery." She stopped at the door and turned back. "Excuse me for asking. But did I hear Lady Harriett's name mentioned? Of course, I was not intentionally eavesdropping, but I heard her name as I approached your study, and it gave me a start. Has she returned?"

Lucas gave a frustrated look. He was certain his mother would have already known this, but this was her way of bringing it out in the open for later discussion. "Yes. It seems *Lady Dudley* is staying with her parents for an undetermined period. I ran into her this afternoon."

"Oh. How wonderful!" She clapped her hands in delight and considered at her son, narrowing her eyes. "I always liked her. Certainly, you realize what happened to her was not her fault. A woman has very little say over these matters . . . as you will soon find out. It is good to know she is around." His mother gave him a knowing wink before turning to leave. "She could prove a helpful resource with your wards," she tutted as she left the room.

A knot caught in his throat at his mother's words. He had considered all of that, but they had been engaged . . . informally, anyway. *Damnit! I will not set myself up for heartache again.* His mother would just have to put aside her predilection for the woman.

"Hiring a governess is an excellent idea," Lucas said, thankful this news had not arrived while his mother was traveling—something she was wont to do lately, now that the war had ended.

As the door closed behind her, Lucas sat in one of the leather chairs around the game table near his friends. "I do not know what I thought the missive contained, but in no way was I prepared for what it said. What do I know about young girls?" he moaned.

"I was only thinking this morning how you might be the only free rascal among us—no responsibilities of marriage and children," Romney said. "Then, the interlude with Lady Harriett occurred, followed by this."

Clarendon snorted.

"This is vexatious! I barely knew my cousin and his wife, and I do not recall meeting these children—*ever*." He pressed his forehead to subdue the headache he could feel starting. He reached for his glass and poured another drink. "Perhaps I should have my man of business look into young women's schools."

"Have a care, man. The young ladies just lost their parents," Clarendon said. "They are being shipped to you. You cannot dispatch them anywhere—at least not so soon."

"You are right. I should find a governess," he said in a beleaguered tone. "I have never looked for a governess before."

"You may find you need to take a wife, as well," teased Romney. "While I offer it in levity, you may find merit in the suggestion. I speak from experience with a very strong-willed sister."

"Hey . . . that is my wife you speak of," objected a laughing Clarendon. "Truth be told, I do not know what I would have done with my son had I not found Charlotte. Certainly, we did not marry for that purpose, but she has added an immeasurable amount of love and peace to my household, not to mention direction that I never thought to find again in my life."

Lucas nodded. "She has made a wonderful wife for you, and to a person, we are very appreciative you found each other," he said. Clarendon had always been one of his dearest childhood friends—even before they went to Eton. When his wife died in childbirth, all of them worried about him. Clarendon lost himself in gambling and drink, while his sister took care of the infant. It was about the time his sister decided Clarendon needed to face his responsibilities and become a father when Lady Charlotte had entered his life. The spitfire had dressed him down at his door for nearly cutting down her younger brother with his carriage while on his way to his club. Their union was a blessing.

Perhaps his friends were right. Maybe he needed to consider a wife. He would give it some thought, although he knew he would never invest his heart again—ever.

"You have made my sister happy," Romney added. "It startled me to return from America and find her married to my best friend, no less. However, I have never entertained a qualm. As long as you are good to her," he said, giving Clarendon a friendly pat on the back.

"I have an idea," offered Clarendon. "Let us ask our wives to create a checklist of things to look for when you interview a governess."

Lucas perked up. "That sounds reasonable."

"Maybe we can offer a few suggestions based on our own experience with governesses," Romney said. "It should make it extremely easy to find if you craft your job requirements. We can have a go at it first. Then, we can turn it over to our wives and your mother for their input."

"A sound idea," Clarendon said, refilling all three glasses. "Whose turn is it to play? We can throw out ideas and the odd man out each game can capture them on paper."

Lucas saw merit in the idea and quickly retrieved paper, a quill, and ink from his desk. "I believe the game is between me and Romney. Clarendon, you start the notes, if you will. We can take turns."

After the day he had already experienced, Lucas felt the activity would be exactly what he needed—laughter, brandy, and his friends. For the next two hours, the men played billiards while they crafted the job description of the perfect governess. He smiled, imagining how the brandy-tinged note-taking had aided in shaping the depiction of what he needed to fill the role.

THEY COULD BE friends?

Friends?

His words rolled around in Harriett's head, increasing the already dull ache she had been nursing since the incident. She had not moved from the parlor settee where Lucas had placed her, insisting she was comfortable. Rather than move, she lay there in introspective silence. She had not wanted to move, but said little to her parents, who had arrived unexpectedly from London while she was out riding. With little regard to her injury, they both seemed more interested, for different reasons, to learn the duke had returned her to their home.

Lucas had returned her home and offered her . . . friendship, with permission to call him *Lucas* in private. The sudden, emotional reminder of all she had lost felt physical as it slammed into her gut. *Was that regret she had seen on her father's face?* Harriett could not be sure. Her father had refused to speak on it again—*it* being his betrayal of his daughter.

She speculated her marriage to Lord Dudley may have caused a rift between her parents, although neither mentioned a word, knowingly, in her presence. They had been a love match and had always treated each other with respect and admiration throughout her early years. After she married, she had begun to notice friction.

Upon her arrival three weeks past, she had overheard her mother pleading with her father to tell her *why* he had pushed their daughter to marry "that despicable man", shortly before they left for London. Her father's response had been curt, telling her to leave it alone and never question his reasons again. His tone had shocked Harriett, who slipped away from the library door, where she had been, unseen. She had come here to see her sister and get away from Kent, not to see her father, although she *had* missed her mother.

Dudley had been despicable. Harriett closed her eyes, trying to force the memories away. "You are my property, gel," he had been fond of saying, before laughing. With a mouth full of rotten teeth, his breath might have wilted a tree.

Mourning him had been an act of pleasure.

There had been no mourning. Rather, she reveled in being able to take a deep lungful of air and not smell the foul odor of his breath near her. She had thrown out all the high-necked dresses she had worn to hide bruises, souvenirs of both his ardor and anger. Instead, she ordered only scoop-necked dresses for mourning. She had worn black as a symbol of survival those first months—not mourning. He had removed her from all she loved.

Worst of all . . . he had taken her from Lucas.

An involuntary shudder overwhelmed her. Their meeting today had been unexpected, but what was even more unimaginable was the coolness he had shown toward her. Harriett knew his voice very well and *his voice told her he was over her.*

A small knock sounded at the door before her mother stepped in. "Darling, we sent for Dr. Thomas. Would you be more comfortable in your room? Or do you wish to stay here? That settee looks so uncomfortable."

"Mama, maybe you are right. I should retire to my room." She moved herself into a sitting position. "I had not expected you and Father to be here. Welcome home."

"Thank you, darling. If you wish to be more comfortable in your bedroom, allow me to have a footman help you upstairs. Wait there," her mother said, then left.

Harriett started to stand up, but her foot nearly gave way. She stayed where she was and waited.

Moments later, her mother returned with Watkins. The burly footman leaned down and picked her up. "Are you comfortable, my lady?" he asked as he walked.

"I am. Thank you," she replied. It felt awkward after having been carried by Lucas.

Once he deposited her on her bed, her mother and maid scurried about her, fluffing her pillow, and helping her into more comfortable clothing.

Jane, her maid, stoked the fire, and within minutes, a roaring fire heated the room. The warmth felt wonderful.

"I have some willow bark tea for the swelling. It should help, my lady."

"Thank you, Jane," Harriett said. She craved solitude. She wanted to feel sorry for herself. And she wanted to lay about in her blue-colored room, draw the pale white draperies closed to allow only the filtered sun, and crawl beneath the soft down of her navy and teal-flowered coverlet and go to sleep.

What she did not want to do was to speak of . . . *him*. The loss felt fresh, again.

"You were about to say how you ran across His Grace," her mother prodded, cradling a warm cup of tea in her hands.

Harriett resisted the impulse to roll her eyes and huff an exasperated breath. "I am not quite sure, Mama. Strangely, my horse got spooked and my foot twisted in the stirrup and pulled me from the seat. I could barely hang on. It must have been my pleas for help, but he came riding up from behind and overtook my horse. The next thing I knew, His Grace had stopped my horse and rescued me."

Her mother smiled at her. "That is a lovely story, my dear."

"Mama. Do not make it more than it was. He stopped my horse and kept my neck in one piece. That is all. He no longer cares for me," Harriett replied. While her head knew this, her heart cried, *no*.

"I am sorry that things did not work out with His Grace when you were courting," her mother murmured. "I will never…"

Harriett let her mother's words fade into silence. As far as she could tell, her mother had no part in what had happened to her on that dreadful day her father introduced her to her *betrothed*. Dudley was a man she had detested for as long as she had known him. He had always seemed the type that pulled wings off butterflies. An impression from her childhood that proved correct, as she found out.

She could ask *why* she had been made to marry him, but having done so for all these years, she knew not to expect an answer. She felt certain her mother did not know *why* Father had consented, either. It seemed destined to remain a mystery. Men expected women to be obedient and not ask questions. They considered women chattel, a notion Harriett detested and one she hoped to see change in her lifetime, while her mother accepted her role.

"I understand, Mother, really, I do," Harriett said, suddenly feeling awash with pain she thought she had buried years past. A deep longing stung her heart and her chest ached with it. Memories and grief were all she had . . . all she could ever have of His Grace, the Duke of Dorman . . . or Lucas Pemberton, as he would always be to her. His were the memories of what *was* so long ago, but could never be again.

"He is still unmarried, Mother," Harriett murmured, fatigued by the futility of the conversation. "At least, that is what I have heard."

"You have kept up with him," observed her mother, sipping her tea.

"Only in passing," Harriett replied. "He is a duke and gossip follows him." Lucas never married, but Harriett knew better than to think he would ever be interested in her again. Her father had seen to that. Inexplicably, she felt a deep sadness toward her father, mingled with ire and a profound sense of loss. He had to have known whom he sent her to marry, yet he still did it.

"It is best we move on, my dear," she said, bussing her cheek with a kiss. "I thought I heard someone arrive. Jane, would you be a dear and check?"

"Yes, milady. I will find out," the older maid said, bobbing a curtesy before leaving the room.

"Was he surprised to see you?" her mother persisted when

the maid had left the room.

Her mother was like a dog with a bone when she wanted to know something. Too bad she had not been this curious when her father had married her off to Dudley. She never referred to her dead husband by his first name—only using the moniker everyone familiar with him used. It irked him when they were at societal events. She often paid a price for her insolence later.

"Yes. He had not expected to see me any more than I expected to see him." It had been difficult.

A tap on the door drew their attention. "Lady Dudley. How do you do?" Dr. Thomas said, standing in the doorway before walking into the room. His father, the elder Dr. Thomas, had delivered her. The younger Dr. Thomas had slowly taken over his father's practice since returning from the war. Old Dr. Thomas often spoke of the letters he received from his son on the battlefield in the Napoleonic campaign. "Good afternoon, Lady Scarsdale," he said, addressing her mother. Turning to his patient, "I hear you have damaged your ankle. May I see it?"

"Yes, doctor." Harriett slowly extended her foot from beneath the cover. She glanced at her foot, noticing the increased swelling.

Thomas slowly turned her ankle in his hand, pressing the swollen areas and coaxing her to move it around at his command. "I believe you sprained your ankle. Stay off it for two weeks and keep it elevated. The pain could become more intense. Willow bark tea can help the swelling and pain." He reached into this bag and withdrew a small bottle. "Laudanum can help with the discomfort and help you sleep."

"Thank you, doctor. I will follow your directions." There was nothing else she could do. She would make it as luxurious as possible. The one good thing about Dudley was his bank account. Thankfully, he had amply provided for her—an unentailed Dudley estate, a considerable sum of money, and a widow's allowance. The remaining properties went to his nephew, who had stepped in and assumed his title. If she never heard her dead husband's voice again, it would be too soon.

Harriett closed her eyes, groggy and hating the heavy after-taste of the sweet opiate the doctor had just given her. She was riding on a horse . . . *but it was his horse. He had saved her.* A pulsing warmth climbed up her back and spread through her loins, ending in her fingers. Its tingling heat felt good, comforting. She could feel his hot breath on her neck. As they turned toward her home, small kisses covered her neck and cheek. His friends rode beside them, but she sensed he did not care. With a moan, his free arm lifted her face toward his, and covered her lips with his own, exploring, warm and familiar as a thick white haze settled over her, separating her from him. A cry ripped from her throat as darkness descended and swallowed her.

CHAPTER THREE

*C*RACK! LUCAS WATCHED the balls scatter across the red felt surface of the billiard table.

"Good break, Clarendon!" Romney exclaimed. "Should we add information about time off for the governess?"

The other two men laughed. "Did your parents give more than the occasional day off for your sister's governess? Two young ladies need to be always watched. My wife—*your sister*—has told me some misadventures of her youth and they rival ours!" Clarendon hooted.

"You make a good point. I should address that!" Lucas snickered. He made a note on the paper, over a hard covered book he used as a lap desk. Their billiard games had devolved into an abundance of levity and good humor. He had needed that. "Let me read what I have." He cleared his throat and read:

GOVERNESS WANTED: Guardian in need of an experienced governess to serve as the female role model of comportment, social behavior, and morality, with skills in the 'feminine' accomplishments (to include languages, art, needlework, and musical achievements), the goal being the preparation of two gently bred young women to take their place in society. Must have suitable references.

"What fine work. It captures your need nicely! Too bad we had to leave off the color of her eyes and the pout of her lips," Clarendon commended. "Perhaps it would be best to discuss holidays and that sort of thing in person."

"You are probably right. Perhaps I will discuss it if the woman brings it up. I honestly do not know what I should consider," Lucas said, drawing a laugh.

"If you let them go first, you may find they ask for very little. It was a trick my father taught me," Romney said with a laugh. "I wonder whether you need to post an advertisement. My parents used to remark on the abundance of ads from women wanting governess positions and would have our man of business pre-screen them. If they found the candidates lacking, he would post the advertisement." Romney aimed his cue stick and took his turn.

Lucas watched Romney's ball kiss another on the table, taking both into the side pocket.

"That's game!" his friend said proudly.

"Romney, you have gotten much better at this than I recalled," Clarendon said with a cough, followed by laughter.

Clarendon looked at Lucas and arched a brow. "A word to the wise. Do not engage your mother in finding this person or you could end up with a young companion for your mother under your roof."

"True, that!" seconded Romney. "I could see my own dear mother resorting to that, had I not found my sweet Bethany. I had not realized so many gently bred women look for these jobs. My sister faced a difficult situation and told me she considered that option herself," Romney said, solemnly. "It was difficult for my family when my father died."

"Your uncle had placed himself in a role of guardian," Clarendon recalled caustically.

"Yes," Lucas agreed. "I cannot believe I have found myself with two wards. What do I know about raising young ladies?"

Romney raised his glass in a feigned salute. "I agree. Although you may know more than you think," he said with a wink.

"I have to disagree. Dorman has made a career of avoiding innocents," Clarendon chuckled, taking the final turn and looking up at his friend. "Now he will have a house full of them."

At that dire warning, Lucas gnashed his teeth and grimly worried that he would soon be over his head in his own house. He needed to hire a governess, and quickly. Reaching up, he tugged the red and gold-colored cord. The door opened and a footman in red livery entered. "Rawlings, ask Mrs. Nettles to send nourishment. Perhaps some cold meats and cheeses. And tell Egerton I need to see him."

"Right away, Your Grace," Rawlings said, bowing as he closed the door.

A few minutes later, Egerton scratched on the door and entered. "Your Grace."

"Egerton. Have Mr. Branson, my man of business, summoned. We need a governess, quickly," he said.

"Immediately, Your Grace," Egerton replied, giving a bow.

Before the older retainer had a chance to close the door, Rawlings appeared with a tray of food. "Mrs. Nettles asked that I tell you she can have a tray of sandwiches prepared, should you require it."

"These are just what we needed," Romney said, helping himself to the cheese and meat.

"I agree," Clarendon said, in between bites.

A quick tap sounded before the duchess sailed into the room. "Darling, I apologize for intruding upon your time together, but I feel some urgency to prepare for the girls' arrival. Mrs. Blaine told me they have made the rooms ready for the young ladies. I have arranged for a wardrobe to be created for them. I shall plan a trip to London to visit my modiste, Madame Trousseau."

"Mother, Romney and Clarendon helped me fashion a job description for a governess," Lucas started.

Romney gave a mocking cough behind him.

Giving his friend a quelling glare, he withdrew the sheet of vellum and offered it to his mother.

The duchess read over it. "You have thought of everything, Lucas. I cannot think of a thing to add to it." She smiled at her son and handed it back. "Unless it is time off," she added quickly.

The men behind him snickered. "We discussed that, Mother. But with two young ladies who we have never met, coupled with . . . *my* limited experience in what to expect, it seems prudent to allow her to bring that up to me. I plan to pay her well, of course."

"Perhaps your plan is clever. It allows you to think about that a bit more," she replied. "I had sisters you know. Raising young ladies will not be so foreign to me. In fact, I look forward to the girls after rearing a house full of young men." She grinned.

A knock sounded at the door and Egerton stepped inside. "Your Grace, a carriage has arrived. I thought you might be expecting it."

HARRIETT AWOKE GROGGY and lay there staring up at the white canopy laced in her favorite navy and teal color combination. She had never planned to sleep the entire afternoon away. However, once she closed her eyes and shut out the world, she felt too comfortable to move. She licked her lips, struggling to hold on to her dream. Only wisps of it remained with her now that she had finally shaken off sleep. She recalled that Lucas had figured prominently in it and there had been no animus—only a calm feeling. Her ankle had finally stopped throbbing, probably after the laudanum had taken effect.

What had started as a simple outing to stretch the legs of her horse had brought her face-to-face with the worst loss of her life. She had loved Lucas. Truth was, she had never stopped. But he had made it clear he no longer returned those feelings.

Dudley had insisted she leave Surrey and any place close to

London, where she would be likely to know people. Her parents had only seen her when they traveled to Kent, which had been rare. This was her first return to Surrey. Harriett had missed it.

Lucas Pemberton still rattled her senses. In her worst moments while married to Dudley, she would close her eyes and imagine Lucas' lips on hers, with the light scruff of his day-long beard against her chin. When she allowed herself, she could return to her last moments with him. He had kissed her lips and leaned his head against hers. "I will speak to your father as soon as he returns," he told her. *That was then.*

Swinging her legs over the side of her bed, she dragged herself up and tested her ankle. There was no way she could stand on it without help.

The door opened, and Jane walked into the room. "Milady, I found a cane for ye to use."

"Your timing is impeccable, Jane," Harriett returned. "I tested my ankle and still feels quite sore."

"Dr. Thomas advised that ye are to stay off it for two weeks," the maid said, arching a brow. "The cane will take some of the weight off of it, when ye 'ave to walk."

Harriett looked at Jane. *Insolent woman*, she thought dryly. As much as she wanted to be upset with her maid, she realized Jane was one reason she had survived these past five years. "I promise not to overexert myself. My sister, Lady Penfield, had promised to visit. Do you know if she has arrived yet?"

"Yer sister arrived about a half-hour ago, my lady. She was visiting with yer mother in the parlor when I came upstairs. I will ask Timmons to bring you downstairs if ye wish to visit there," Jane offered.

"We can put Timmons off for a little while, Jane. I decided to visit my sister in her room. And I come bearing gifts—it seems the perfect gift, considering," Lady Penfield said, her petticoat rustling about her as she entered the room. She placed a covered basket on the floor next to the bed. "Would you be so good as to bring us some chocolate and biscuits, Jane?" she asked.

Jane nodded. "Yes, miladies."

As the door closed behind Jane, Harriett turned to her sister. "Alice, why are you so wicked to my maid? Without her, I might have lost my sanity these past years."

"She never loses control, Harriett. I consider it a challenge to provoke her," her sister replied nonchalantly.

"That is hardly a reason to harass my maid," Harriett returned angrily.

"Relax. I have nothing against her, really. Excepts she purses her lips whenever she sees me, like she disdains me or I smell," her sister said with a sneer. "Besides, I came to see you, not Jane."

"Alice! I like Jane. She is good to me—*always*. Try to remember that she was all I had with me when things were hard," Harriett said, exasperated with her younger sister. "Now, what did you bring me?" She pointed towards the basket, softening her voice.

"Meet Penelope," her sister said, opening the basket. A black puppy with white markings on her left ear, toes, and tail-tip emerged.

"Ruff," the puppy protested, slowly straightening her legs and exiting the basket. She walked to the pillow next to Harriett and stretched out before she stood and walked to Harriett.

"It is nice to meet you, Penelope," Harriett said, scratching the pup's chin with an index finger.

"She is yours if you want her. Daisy had a litter of two about eight weeks ago. This one has a very independent personality. She reminded me of you, so I offer her to you," Alice said proudly.

Upon hearing her name, Penelope stood up and batted her big grey eyes before rubbing against Harriett's out-stretched arm. "And when you asked, what did Mother say about a dog in the house?" Harriett asked.

"Mother said your duke brought you home," Alice returned, obviously ignoring the question.

"He is not *my* duke. Not anymore," Harriett replied. "My foot had gotten caught in my stirrup. I am still not sure how that happened." She sighed. "He and his friends were, I guess, heading home. They saw my horse bolting and came to my rescue."

"We are all fortunate you were not hurt worse than an ankle sprain. Although our mother is still caught up in discussing your daring rescue," Alice derided.

"Yes. I know."

"Father was in the parlor when I arrived. I am not sure what they were discussing, but he left when Mother told me about your rescue," Alice added. "He always wears such a pained expression when the duke's name comes up. It was the same as when he was a mere marquess. When you left, he bade us all not to bring up his name."

"Interesting," Harriett murmured.

A small knock on the door preceded the entry of a maid carrying a tray and a small pitcher. "Milady, Miss Jane said you requested chocolate and biscuits."

"Thank you, Tammy. Please place them on the table, there," Harriett said, pointing to a small table sitting between two white-upholstered, mahogany armchairs in front of the fireplace.

"Yes, milady," the maid said before placing the tray on the small, Chippendale table and leaving.

"This bedroom suits you, dear sister," Alice said, standing and walking to a chair. "It is elegant but understated. Exactly as I have always thought of you." She looked around. "I have never been to your home in Kent, but I always imagined it exactly like this—vivacious and light-filled."

"Thank you, Alice." She smiled at her sister, as she often did when she did not have a suitable response. Alice had always been more observant and unafraid of speaking about her feelings. Growing up, she had vexed their mother to no end. It had been quite the surprise when she achieved a match for her first Season with one of the most sought-after young men. The Earl of Penfield and her sister were a love match.

It was exactly as Harriett had wanted.

Instead, her father had consigned her to . . . Dudley, who had felt he should be esteemed by all he came into contact with, yet had, himself, little regard for others. Thinking of him always made her think her life had become a sick fairytale. She struggled to avoid any reminders of him; yet seeing Lucas today had brought everything back—the feelings she had buried of her long-ago love, as well as the fresh pain of being married off to satisfy a debt and losing her hope of happiness. *Foolish woman!* How could she have thought to visit her home and not run into the man?

"Are you not going to tell me?" Alice said, as she adjusted herself in the chair next to her sister.

"Tell you . . . what?" Harriett replied, pretending ignorance. She did not want to talk about him. Yet, she knew that until she somehow closed the door, questions would plague her . . . especially from her sister Alice, who had always been her biggest champion.

"Do not be coy, Harriett. It does not become you," answered Alice, leaning in to pour their chocolate from the china teapot. "I really do enjoy chocolate. It was a habit you got me started on, you know." She set the pot down and cocked her head toward Harriett, clearly waiting for her sister's response.

"I do not know what to say," started Harriett. "He rescued me, but knowing Lucas . . . I mean *His Grace*, it is what one would have expected from him."

"You called him . . . Lucas," remarked Alice astutely.

"Please do not read something where there is nothing. There can be nothing. He said as much before he left."

"What do you mean?" asked Alice, arching a brow.

"He said we could be *friends,*" blurted Harriett in disdain, before taking a sip.

"*Now* who is reading something where there could be nothing?" answered her sister, meaningfully, before taking a slow sip of her chocolate. She fixed her gaze on her sister. "There could be so much more than *friendship.*"

CHAPTER FOUR

The next day
Pembley Manor

"**Y**OUR GRACE, YOUR mother, Her Grace, has requested to see you in her chambers—before you go down to break your fast, if possible," Wilson said as he pulled Lucas' cravat into a mathematical tie.

"One day I will learn that particular knot, Wilson," Lucas said with a laugh. "I have tried to reconstruct it, but to no avail." He ran a hand through his hair. "Did Mother mention anything so it might prepare me for what awaits?" She seemed to delight in his discomfiture around the girls. They had arrived the evening before. The staff had taken to them immediately, not having had children in the home since his youngest brother, Taylor, left for Eton. Since their arrival, on top of the day he had already had yesterday, his life felt completely upended.

"She did not, Your Grace. As far as the tie goes. You are not to worry. That is why you have me. It is my pleasure," Wilson said as he helped Lucas into a navy superfine wool jacket over a muted gold waistcoat.

Lucas stepped in front of his mirror and admired Wilson's work. Romney and Clarendon planned to join him downstairs shortly and ride out to Epsom with him. He had planned to leave before the young ladies woke up. "If I thought it would work, I would double your wages to tell my mother you missed me," he laughed.

Wilson gave a sly smile. "I would take you up on that if it had a chance. Her Grace would never believe it."

The two of them laughed.

"Yes. It is always best to give her her way," Lucas agreed. He walked down the hall and knocked on his mother's suite of rooms, mentally preparing for what, he was not sure.

The door swung open. "Darling, come in." She patted the place next to her on the velour window seat.

Rather than sit, he stood, receiving a subtle, probing glance from his mother.

"I was just discussing what is needed for our two newest family members, Beatrice and Catherine. I believe a trip into Town in the next day or two to see the modiste shall be necessary," she explained.

"Will Mrs. Stewart be joining you?" He glanced around for the girls' aunt, who had arrived last evening with them.

"Aunt Esther is still abed, after our long trip," volunteered Miss Beatrice.

"Yes, poor dear. I have ordered food to be brought to her room. It was an extremely long trip. The woman contends she must leave tomorrow. While I encouraged her to take a few days to recover, she insists. Her driver is resting in one of the stable rooms. I asked Cook to prepare a basket for their return trip," his mother added.

"You have thought of everything," he said. "As usual, Mother, planning is your specialty."

She preened under the praise. "It is a hostess' duty to ensure her guests are well provided for," she began.

"You can call me Cat," the youngest one interjected, grinning. "All my friends do, and we will be friends, won't we?"

His mother cleared her throat. "My dear, my son is a *duke*, and one should address him as Your Grace, until he gives you leave to do otherwise. And," she took a calming breath, "a young lady *does not* interrupt in a conversation."

"Oh. I apologize, Your Grace," she said cheekily. "Anyway, you may call me Cat."

Lucas arched a brow and bit back a smile. "I am pleased to know that, Miss Catherine. And I am certain we will be friends."

His young ward beamed.

For whatever reason, Lucas liked the chit, even though a small voice inside screamed she would be trouble. He made a mental note to find a governess soon—the sooner, the better. However, his mother had taken the two girls on temporarily, which could prove entertaining—a test of wills, so to speak.

He cleared his throat. "You are speaking of Richmond, I assume," he remarked, making sure they had not intended to go to London. One never knew about his mother. With a moment's notice, she might pack her bags and go off visiting friends. Since his father's death, it seemed she had become more adventurous. Using *that* term in reference to his mother made him unexplainably nervous.

"Not today. I thought we would meet with Mrs. Thimblesby in Richmond. She does excellent work, although she does not have access to the same selection of fabric available to Madame Trousseau in London. We shall plan an adventure in London in a few months. I should like to have Beatrice outfitted for her to come out to Society during the little Season. I have planned a trip to Richmond once the girls have a day or two to rest."

Lucas noticed Catherine roll her eyes from behind his mother and her sister at the mention of her sister's launch into Society. She froze when she realized he had seen her. Perhaps there was a little sibling rivalry, at least for the younger sister. He would bear it in mind.

"Aunt Esther feels we have all we need for now," said Beatrice. "I helped her dye our dresses for the mourning period."

"Mother, how do you plan to address the mourning period?" he asked. Cat was wearing pink and Beatrice was in a black dress that looked too small. He was certain his mother would handle it, but needed to understand her thinking because the Season started in less than three months—or that is when she had originally planned to return to London—and she had already mentioned having dresses made.

"I have given that some thought and feel six months would be better than the year, particularly given their ages," she explained, giving a covert glance at Cat. "I will have Mrs. Thimblesby fashion clothing to accommodate the need. Aunt Esther had several of their dresses dyed black, but they are being cleaned after the long trip."

"I see. Order what you need, Mother," he agreed. As the girls' parents had been distant relations to both him and his mother, there had been no formal mourning required. The girls had been away at school and with all the shuffling they had been forced to endure, he wanted them made comfortable.

"Thank you, Your Grace," both girls said, together.

Things were going to get interesting around here. He sensed it. "Mother, I am traveling to Epsom to look over a horse that the Regent is selling. It's a grey and I believe it could add a lot to my chances to race."

"A grey has never won the Derby," his mother intoned. "Who are the parents?"

Mother never failed to amaze him with her interests beyond what he thought most women had. That had always been the case growing up. "It is interesting that you ask that. I had forgotten you and Father frequented the Derby. You may remember the horse. The Regent sired one of his grey mares with the Derby winner from 1807, and a full brother to the Epsom Derby winners, Paris, and Archduke sired the dam."

"Does the seller know this?" his mother asked, obviously shocked.

"Possibly. However, he made it known he no longer wants the animal. And I am most eager to attain the horse. The person who purchased him is not thrilled and plans to sell the little grey. I want to get him before someone else does it. Perhaps there could be a two-year, or a three-year season for the colt," he said.

"I wish I could go with you, Your Grace," Cat piped up.

His mother gave a forced smile as she shot a quelling glance in the girl's direction.

"Do you know much about horseflesh, Cat?" he asked, acknowledging her requested name.

This time *his mother* rolled her eyes, registering her disapproval in a quiet reprimand to his use of the child's shortened name. She detested nicknames for young women, although Lucas felt this one fit the girl nicely. "You cannot attend this trip, poppet," he said. "My friends and I intend to make it a fast one. If I purchase the animal, he shall live here, and you shall have plenty of time to know him. Do you ride?"

"Papa and Mama taught Bea and me to ride. Mama allowed us to ride astride when we were at our country home, but made us learn sidesaddle," Cat replied.

"I am glad I asked. I shall ensure you have saddles to ride," he said with a wink, much to his mother's dismay. The more he spoke with the girl, the more he liked her—even so, he realized with more certainty that she would be a handful. He hoped for an excellent governess who would train her in the things she needed to know without breaking her spirit. He had not been around sisters, but he enjoyed the girl's pluck. "If there is nothing else, Mother, we shall return later, but we plan to stop both ways at The Blue Boar to rest the horses, as usual."

"Thank you for letting me know, Son. Good luck on the purchase," his mother said, and turned to Cat. "Girls, perhaps we should break our fast and spend time making a list for our upcoming shopping trip. Town is fairly close, but shopping for dresses can be tedious." The duchess turned back to her son. "I look forward to meeting this grey. His father was a beautiful horse. It should be fun to watch him come into his own," she said with a grin.

Both girls curtsied before leaving the room, followed by his mother. He would speak to Egerton on the way out and have him place an advertisement for the governess, directing candidates to Branson for the initial assessment. It would ensure more candidates. He could already tell his mother would need a break . . . soon.

⇥⟫⟪⇤

"WAKE UP, DEAR sister," implored Alice. "I need to stretch my legs and wondered if you might join me for a ride?"

Harriett sat up in her bed and stretched, glancing out the window. The sun looked much higher than its usual position when she awoke. She had overslept. "Why did Jane let me sleep so long?" she complained.

"Apparently you needed it! That disgusting laudanum added to it, I am sure. If you can do without that, it would be best. I awake with the worst headache if I use it," Alice contended.

"That explains my achy head. Perhaps willow bark tea would suffice. Doctor Thomas warned me about the laudanum." Harriett begrudgingly pushed back the coverlet and swung her legs over the side of the bed. Sitting up helped her head clear.

"Jane seems to have expected that. She brought you the willow bark tea, your chocolate and a couple of biscuits. I would suggest we have the biscuits and chocolate, first. Then the willow bark tea may not be so bad," Alice suggested.

"We?" Harriett said, grinning.

"Of course! I have mine over here. Let me assist you with the chairs. I would own these are the finest sitting chairs in the house!" Alice exclaimed.

"My foot does not have the steady throb of yesterday . . ." she said, gingerly placing her foot on the ground with her weight on it. "Ouch! It still hurts. Perhaps the willow bark tea is just what I need. I will have it first. Would you assist me?"

Harriett leaned into Alice for support and hobbled to the

cushy seat in front of her. Sitting, she exhaled a deep, whooshing breath. Once settled, she sipped her willow bark tea until the dregs in the cup's bottom stared back at her. Dispensing with the cup, she propped her foot on the footstool in front of her and took a bite of a biscuit. Minutes ticked by while both women quietly sipped their chocolate and ate the biscuits until Harriett recalled what her sister had asked of her and stopped.

"Did you ask me to ride horses with you? That's what got me into this mess! Are you mad?"

"You know I am," her sister grinned, never moving from her comfortable position on the chair. "However, I brought you something." Alice reached underneath her chair and pulled out a brass cane she had hidden. "Jane helped me find it. It used to be Grandmama's!"

"Oh, my goodness! I have not seen that in an age . . . well, since Grandmama passed away. I can still see her bearing down on it and making her way around." Harriett hesitated and nibbled at her lower lip. "Do you think it will work?"

"There's nothing like trying it and finding out," Alice suggested. "Stand up and try to walk. Not too much, mind you, until you get accustomed to it. However, it may keep you from being carried up and downstairs by Timmons," she teased with a sly grin.

"Yes. That was most embarrassing. It might relegate me to that for days to come," she lamented, with a feigned pathetic look on her face.

Her sister broke out in laughter. "He *is* so handsome. I was jealous, you know, and began imagining all the places he could carry me. But if I mention them, it would be my luck that Mother would walk in, hear me, and swoon on the spot!"

The two of them dissolved into girlish giggles. It had been a long time since Harriett had laughed that hard, she realized. She always enjoyed Alice's company. Her sister always made her feel better.

Harriett nibbled her lower lip and reached for the cane. Slowly, she pulled herself up, doing her best to distribute her weight between the cane and her uninjured leg. Her feet felt a little wobbly and sore, but the important thing was she could stand, she thought, smiling in triumph. "It works wonderfully! Alice, you are a genius," she effused.

"I should take the credit. However, Mother mentioned it yesterday, and Jane found it."

"I suppose we can ride the horses if I do it astride. I would hate to have anything like what happened yesterday happen again. I hope Mother understands," Harriett said.

"I would not ask Mother. She will have you in bed for the duration of these two weeks—not to mention her reaction to your plan to ride astride!" Alice stooped down and looked at Harriett's ankle. "Your foot does not even appear swollen, and the dark bruise is the only way you can tell you injured it."

"Right! Mother would be overly cautious. Can you help me dress?" The idea of riding her mare appealed to her. Her injury had curtailed her ride yesterday. "My riding habit is in the closet. Jane brushed it out."

"The purple velvet one?" Alice asked, reaching into the wardrobe and fingering the fabric between her fingers. "I love that color on you. It will be lovely."

"Thank you. I had it made shortly before leaving Kent. Once the mourning period ended, I commissioned all new clothes and left," Harriett said, suddenly feeling a little restrained.

"From what you've told me, Harriett, I can certainly understand," her sister whispered. She walked back and hugged Harriett. "Let us get you dressed. It is time to have some fun!"

An hour later, Harriett and Lady Alice mounted their horses in front of the house. Harriett changed her mind about riding astride when she realized the level of help she would need from Timmons to sit in the seat. He attached the cane to her saddle.

"I have not ridden in an age. It feels wonderful!" Alice exclaimed, as the wind pulled the pins from her hair. "How do you feel?"

"Better than I thought I would." Harriett glanced back over her shoulder. "Timmons is staying behind. I think he believes I shall slide from the seat. I will do my utmost to disappoint," she said, chuckling. "As long as we do not run into a shower, we should be fine."

"Let us take the road. I do not want to take a chance of running up on uneven ground," Harriett suggested.

Her sister nodded and the two women set out to let the horses stretch their legs, Harriett not caring her hairpins were flying from their hair. Her loose blonde tresses swirled around her neck and her chin, giving her a feeling of freedom that she had not felt in a long while. They rounded a corner and met three men on horseback. As they drew closer, she slowed, suddenly unsure of what to do. It was Lucas and his friends . . . and they were coming to a stop.

CHAPTER FIVE

"LADY DUDLEY, LADY Penfield!" Lucas tipped his hat, eyeing the beauties in front of him. What in the world was she doing on her horse? He noticed the footman . . . Timmons, if he recalled correctly, keeping a respectful distance, and waiting under a shade tree.

"Your Grace," Alice said. "What a surprise." She glanced over at her sister. "My mother mentioned you were back in Town."

"It's nice to see you again, Your Grace," Harriett added.

"Lady Dudley. How is your ankle?" he asked, pointedly moving his eyes towards her stirrups.

"Better. The swelling has gone down considerably, although I fear I shall walk with a decided limp for a few days," she replied.

"I can certainly understand," he said. "I am relieved to know your injury was only a simple sprain. Your foot was tangled in the stirrup, and you were barely hanging onto your horse. I wondered if something had spooked her." He nodded, indicating her horse, who was quietly munching the grass beneath her, unfazed by the company of the gentlemen and the additional horses.

Lucas noticed a blush creep up her neck and fought the impulse to feel sorry for her. He fought the impulse to feel anything when in her presence, which was distracting. He tried not to notice how beautiful she looked with her long blonde hair that appeared to have been restyled by the wind. Finding himself focused on her full lips, Lucas shifted his gaze away, pretending to observe the surrounding area. The last thing he needed—or wanted—was to get entangled with her again. He had moved on—or thought he had. And he needed to do so again. He touched the brim of his hat. "We should be on our way, as someone is meeting us in Epsom." Glimpsing her deep green eyes, he thought he recognized sorrow. He looked at Lady Alice Penfield. Ladies, it was a pleasure, of course."

His two friends followed, and the three men rode away, leaving Harriett, her sister, and their footman behind them.

"At the risk of your considerable ire over this topic, that seemed rather curt," Romney gently chastised.

"Do not . . ." Lucas started but stopped. "You are right. It was not well done of me. However, in my defense, it took me years to get past the hurt. And here she is again . . . and she is available."

"And?" Clarendon asked.

"And . . . nothing." Lucas bit off. "I plan to avoid her as much as possible."

"As you recall, I allowed the pain of loss to rule my life for years. And while our losses are not the same, what is similar is the *possibility* of love—*of happiness*—being ignored in favor of the pain. I am not saying you should open your heart to a repeat of what was. However, while I mourned my horrific loss—and became comfortable in my alternative life of drinking and gaming—my infant son was ignored, and I can never get back the time I spent drunk or punishing myself. Time is something that, once gone, cannot be replaced."

"Profound, my friend," grinned Romney, riding close and slapping Clarendon on the back.

"We are not speaking of the same thing, Clarendon," huffed Lucas, feeling irritated. His friend was right about time being lost—but he was not willing to concede. No way was he willing to get involved with Lady Harriett Dudley. He would never forget his last conversation with her father and did not think he could ever forgive him.

"It is none of my business. But I do wish to see you happy, my friend," Clarendon allowed.

"I can appreciate that, but your life was different. You had a wife that died in childbirth. We all understood your need to escape the pain. To a person, we found it hard watching you slipping into the void of alcohol and gaming."

Clarendon looked his way and nodded. "Thank you. Mercifully, my sister demanded better of me and shook me from my reverie."

"Hell's teeth! She twisted her ankle and was out riding it today, as if nothing had happened," Lucas growled. Rescuing her had kept him awake most of the night thinking about her. He refused to go down that path again. *Did she have no care for her health?*

"Perhaps her ankle has significantly healed," Romney offered.

Lucas scowled in his friend's direction. "I am no longer concerned with her."

"I can see that," Clarendon muttered in a low voice.

"When did Lady Alice marry? I may have been away when it happened, for I do not recall the event," inquired Romney, sounding jovial and evidently attempting to change the subject. "Obviously, I still have catching up to do."

Clarendon snorted, which caused Lucas to laugh, and he realized the need to change his disposition.

"She stepped outside of propriety and was forced to marry. However, my darling wife feels they are a love match, and simply took matters into their own hands," Clarendon added. "They appear to dote on one another when in public."

"She always struck me as a shrewd one," laughed Romney. "Perhaps marriage agrees with her."

"I would say you have also done well, my friend," Lucas said cheerfully. He was truly happy for Romney. The man had been to Hell and back, and somehow found a wonderful woman on his path back to life. He had heard about the casualties suffered in New Orleans during that last battle of the war and was glad not to have lost his friend.

"Will we be bringing the grey back?" Clarendon asked.

"No. We shall meet my ostler and a stablehand who will transport the horse. I thought that might be best."

"Good thinking. The ride is only a few hours," agreed Romney. "And the sooner you get him in your stable, the better."

Lucas nodded and nudged his steed into a faster canter and his friends followed. An hour-and-a-half later, they rode into the courtyard of *The Blue Boar* and handed their mounts over to the stablehand. The building was a rambling affair of add-on buildings built around a three-story central structure, all made of rough-hewn timbers and white-washed brick. A massive oak in the courtyard separated the main building from the unattached stables to its right. Today, it felt good to feel the coolness of the shade.

"Give them a good rubdown and have the smithy check their shoes," Clarendon said, giving several shillings to the ostler. "There will be more when we leave."

"Yes, milords," he said with a slight bow, before gathering the three horses and leading them to the stable.

The three men walked to the door and were greeted by the innkeeper and his wife. "Your Grace, it is wonderful to see you," gushed Mr. Harry, the innkeeper.

"We appreciate the opportunity to fill our bellies and warm ourselves, Mr. Harry. You and your wife keep a most pleasant establishment," Lucas said in acknowledgement.

The innkeeper turned to his wife. "Martha, take His Grace to the private room and have a maid stoke the fireplace."

His wife nodded and hurried to do her husband's bidding.

"Today's special is mutton, leeks and potatoes, Your Grace. Make yourselves comfortable and I will bring a pitcher of ale for you," the innkeeper added.

"That sounds perfect! Lead the way."

ONCE THE SHOCK of seeing Harriett and her sister passed, Lucas found the trip to Epsom good fun. They arrived at the stable area for the Epsom Downs Racecourse just as the horse and its current owner arrived. The transaction took very little time. He had already decided to make the purchase, convinced he was getting the better end of the deal.

"You are getting an excellent deal, Your Grace," the man said, accepting the money and signing the bill of sale.

"I am positive of that, Lord Ripley," Lucas returned, accepting the bill of sale and the horse. He shook the man's hand and took the reins of the horse. As he led the horse away with his friends, he whispered to the horse. "I think I am getting the better end." Lucas snickered and tucked the bill of sale in the breast pocket of his coat. "We need to celebrate," he said as he walked up to his friends.

"I wish you were not my friend," Romney joked. "I would have attempted to outbid you on that horse."

Lucas smirked and lifted a brow. "That would merely have driven the price up for me, my friend, and you would have to pay for our small celebration," he retorted, giving a feigned look of irritation.

Clarendon clapped him on the back. "Perhaps we should celebrate when we are closer to home. *The Blue Boar* will welcome the coin and if we get a little out of control, we can stay."

Lucas gave a startled look and quickly schooled his features so as not to embarrass his friend. Even though Evan had cut back his drinking, he had not realized his friend's measure of reform. "That might be wise," he returned. "We should feel comfortable letting our hair down."

"I guess my dear Charlotte has really settled you, my friend," Romney put in.

Clarendon smiled. "Your sister is a jewel, believe me. I make it a point *not* to disappoint her."

"Indeed," Lucas agreed. "I cannot recall a time where we have deferred celebratory libations," he added with a chuckle. A pang of jealousy hit him from nowhere. He had never thought to be the only one of his closest friends, still unmarried. Seeing Harriett earlier had been unexpected. Who was he kidding? Seeing her at all had been unexpected . . . and unnerving. He had loved her, and the loss still stung, as much as he had hoped to be well past that pain.

The three of them reached the stabled area where their horses were being cared for. Once they were underway, they rode in silence for a couple of miles before anyone spoke. Lucas had become lost in thought about his new venture. The grey had not cost nearly what Mr. Ripley could have commanded for it. The steed's lineage alone set him head and shoulders above others. He recalled hearing about the opportunity by accident, having overheard Ripley speak of it at White's when he had last been in London. With only a few exchanges since, a deal had been struck, and the meeting decided upon. Ripley had gaming debts to pay and was anxious to raise the money—and while Lucas knew this, he did not allude to it. Rather, he had allowed the man to name his price, which turned out to be much lower than he could have expected. And indeed, the man seemed thrilled to gain what he perceived as his asked-for price.

"You are going to race him, aren't you?" Romney said. It was more of a statement than a question.

"I am," Lucas said matter-of-factly.

"You must promise to tell us when," Clarendon inserted. "My bride mentioned an interest in attending a horserace at Epsom. To know a contender would thrill her."

"I doubt Bethany has ever witnessed one. She may enjoy attending as well. If she does not perceive the animals are mistreated, we would have a chance of keeping her seated," he laughed.

"I would feel the same way," Lucas said, as the three of them rode up to the stables of The Blue Boar and Lucas reined in his mount. Once he dismounted, he stretched his long legs as he waited for his friends to dismount. Two stablehands rushed out to meet them, taking the horses' reins.

"Brush them, water them and feed them lightly. We do not have much further to go," Lucas said, tossing both boys a coin.

"Aye, m'lord," the taller one said without hesitation, taking the silver coin and biting it.

Lucas smiled at the lad and passed each another coin. He never understood the need to bite the coin. Shaking his head, he watched his friends add additional coin to the boys' hands, adding their appreciation for the boys' hard work.

"Gads, Lucas! I am as stiff as a board. I need to ride more," Romney complained, stretching slightly, and mopping his brow.

His tall, dark-headed friend stood and smiled, in good humor, as always. "I would welcome your participation in the training, friend," Lucas offered.

As they approached the door to the inn, it opened and the short, squarish innkeeper greeted them. "Welcome back, Your Grace! I have reserved the private room for you and your friends!" He indicated they should follow.

They walked into a dark paneled room lit by the roaring fire. Each of the well-hewn, oaken walls held a wall sconce with a brace of five candles. The slate stone floor was clean and covered by a worn, red rug.

"Let us grab some food and drink, men," Clarendon said. "I am starving, and kidney pie sounds delicious."

They had barely taken their chairs when the door flew open, and a young woman entered carrying a steaming tray of food. "I'll be back w'ye port, m'lords," she said laying out the plates and utensils.

The barmaid was not uncomely. She was short with a pale complexion and red hair. A smile lit her face as she cast a knowing glance at Romney and Clarendon, registering their obvious discomfort. "Would m'lords require anything else?"

"N . . .no, that will be all for now, miss," Romney stammered.

"Pity," she said, giving an exaggerated wink before leaving the room.

When the door closed, Lucas guffawed, slapping his friend on the back. "Perhaps I should look around for a betting book," he teased.

"I see where that is going. I had nothing to do with placing that bet at your club," Romney protested.

Lucas glanced at Clarendon, who sat smirking from across the table, arms akimbo. "I will uncover who posted the wager," he said pointedly, determined not to smile.

"Tell us more about the grey," Romney suggested, claiming a healthy portion of the kidney pie, before passing the bowl to Clarendon.

The maid entered again, carrying a tray of glasses and a bottle of port. She placed the beverage on the table and gave each man a glass, pausing at Romney and smiling. "I will bring more if 'tis your desire, m'lord," she said meaningfully, before leaving the room.

Lucas winked at his friend. "Perhaps she recognizes you from the Society sheets when you returned from your American adventure," he suggested.

Clarendon snorted.

Romney chuckled. "Have your fun. Your turn will come." He looked at both men, purposely.

"Let us get back to the grey. I am intrigued by the effort you went to, to gain him," said Clarendon. "I believe you may have added a star to your stable."

"Have you followed the Prince Regent's famous house of grey mares at Hampton House?" Lucas asked.

"Of course!" said Clarendon, scraping his chair as he pulled it closer. "Is this horse related?"

"Yes. The horse has an illustrious history already. The Prince Regent bred him. His sire was the 1807 derby winner. And as if that were not enough, they sired his dam by the brother of two Epsom Derby winners—Paris and Archduke," Lucas stated proudly. "I am inspired by his lineage."

"Did the seller not recognize the pedigree of the horse?"

Romney quizzed.

Lucas shrugged. "Lord Ripley did not seem to care," he said. "He made known he wished to rid himself of the animal at the club, and I was lucky enough to overhear. I took him up on it. Twenty-five guineas were a small enough price to gain this level of horseflesh."

"Are you kidding? It was a steal!" exclaimed Clarendon. "I cannot wait to see this little fellow after you have run him through his paces."

"You must have known something," Romney said, grinning at his friend.

"Not at the time," Lucas admitted. "He mentioned he had purchased the horse from Hampton Court. When I ran into the Prince Regent, later, I asked him about the colt and he gave me more detail, curious to hear that the colt was being resold. With his lineage, I think he has a shot at the title."

"What are you going to name him?" Clarendon asked.

"What do you think of Colton?" Lucas asked. He sipped his port and watched his friends mull the name over. "I am thinking of a renaming the colt."

"I like it," Romney said, setting his glass down and refilling it. "Very creative."

"Me too," added Clarendon. "What do you have in mind for Colton?"

"I want to see how his training comes along. If he is ready, I plan to see how he does as a two-year-old in the July derby."

A loud commotion in the tavern's front drew their attention. Lucas heard Mr. Harry explaining his policy not to disclose the names of his patrons. A man was demanding directions to Canton Manor. *How could he not know how to get there? That was the Earl of Scarsdale's home.* "Excuse me, gentlemen. I will see if I can be of help in the front." The men looked at each other.

"Do you think you will need our help?" Romney asked.

"No. If things get loud, maybe then lend a hand," Lucas laughed. "I may have recognized a voice out here."

Both men nodded acceptance. With that, Lucas opened the door to the main room of the tavern. Seeing Mr. Harry still arguing, he walked up to the two men.

"Mr. Harry, I heard raised voices and wondered if you needed some help. I rarely get involved, but I heard Lord Scarsdale's name mentioned," Lucas supplied. He did not feel easy about interfering, yet he had never lost the feeling that something was amiss with Harriett's father. He was not sure what he would find out, but he could not seem to control his need to try.

"Your Grace," Mr. Harry began. "This gentleman says he has a delivery for Lord Scarsdale . . . actually, one of his daughters . . . and I suppose I overreacted to the unusual request. We are not exactly neighbors, but it is not infrequent that we get occasional requests for directions. However, I am not of the practice of directing strangers to the daughter of an earl."

"I see," Lucas said. "That is a good practice you have. As I am also a neighbor, of sorts, I am appreciative."

"Well, yes, Your Grace! You are a valued client and friend, if I may be so bold," gushed Mr. Harry. "I would not be directing every Tom, Dick, and Harry to your doorstep," he promised.

Lucas wanted to know more about the business this man was about, but it was imperative he take his time with this. "May I inquire as to the nature of the business you have with . . . *which daughter* did you say?" he asked.

"I did not say, Yer Grace," the tall, burly man answered, now crossing his arms. His scruffy appearance matched his gruff voice, and his tone had become irritated. "I am not accustomed to the roads here in your county and got turned around. I have traveled from Kent and need to relay a missive to Lady Harriett Dudley, and I understand she is Lord Scarsdale's daughter." The dark-haired man glared at Lucas and Mr. Harry.

"Ah. Lady Dudley. Could I be of help and deliver it for you?" Lucas asked, wincing inside at the forwardness of his request. His mother would be shocked, despite his ducal status. *What was it about Harriett that caused him to lose all grasp of his good sense? Still?*

"I thank ye, but I was told to put the note in the lady's hands directly, *Yer Grace*," the man replied, barely suppressing a sneer. "If yer not going to tell me where the estate is, I will ask in Town. I had hoped not to go beyond where I needed to go, as I have been riding since Kent." The man placed the folded paper back in a small leather pouch, which he returned to his pocket. He patted his pocket and closed his jacket. "I will be on my way. Good day, Yer Grace," he said, deciding to leave and turning around.

"Wait," Lucas said, stopping him. "Harry, I see no harm in directing him to Lady Dudley's home, although I appreciate your efforts as discretion. I will let Lord Scarsdale know the next time I speak to him." *Which would be . . . never.* He could not imagine ever having anything to say to the man. In the limited times he had been forced to be in the same room as the earl, particularly since his father's death, it had not escaped his notice that the earl avoided looking at him.

"Thank you, Your Grace. On your recommendation, I will direct him. Please rejoin your friends and continue to relax in the private dining room."

Lucas wished he could have asked more of the stranger, but good sense finally prevailed, and his usual more ascetic decorum took over.

When he returned to the dining room, both of his friends looked up at him.

"Were you able to resolve the issue, my friend?" Romney asked.

"I was. The chap needed directions to Canton Manor. Mr. Harry had refused, out of neighborly concern, but I assured him Scarsdale would not mind."

"Interesting," Clarendon said. "Did he mention the intended recipient? I heard Kent discussed."

"You know that would have been vulgar of me to ask such a thing . . ." Lucas started.

"Yet you did," Romney said with a sly grin on his face. The two men looked at him expectantly.

Lucas hung his head and shook it, chuckling. "God help me . . . I could not resist." He had to laugh, or he would cry. This woman still had the power five years later to upend him.

"It is obvious there is still feeling for this woman," Romney said gently. "Perhaps you owe it to yourself to . . ."

"No. I will not put myself through that again. You know how upset I was—what I went through," Lucas returned sternly.

"I do," Romney said simply. "But I also know it was not her fault, as do you."

"She never told me he died. Never reached out to me," Lucas said, sounding wounded and ashamed.

"What would you have her say?" Clarendon asked. "I went through hell when Amelia died," he said, pausing. "I even gave my child to my sister to care for. I blamed everyone for something that had nothing to do with anything but fate. Had Charlotte not pushed her way past all of my bluster, I may have missed out on life—at least a happy life."

"Clarendon is right, Pemberton. If you continue to look for reasons to keep the wound festering, you are bound to find them. Losing my sight for a time taught me to pay more attention to what mattered around me," Romney chimed in. "At least talk to Lady Dudley. Her father be damned, but give *her* a chance to help you close that wound."

It all made sense to him. And he knew he should listen. His heart tugged at him. But his mind kept replaying that last meeting with Lord Scarsdale. He shook his head. "I do not know that I can do it."

Both men nodded understanding. "Give yourself time. Perhaps an opportunity will present itself," Romney suggested quietly.

Lucas nodded and picked up his glass of port. "To friends— brothers, really," he toasted.

"Hear, hear!" his friends replied, clinking their glasses up before turning them up and drinking them dry.

CHAPTER SIX

The next day

"CAT, IT IS time to rise. Mr. Whitesides will be here soon for your piano lessons. This day begins early!" The duchess walked over to Catherine's bed and squeezed her toes, an affectionate gesture she had probably learned from her own parents. She did it to her boys when they were young, on those days she would wake them.

"Who is Mr. Whitesides?" Cat asked, sitting up and struggling to wipe the sleep from her eyes.

"The pianoforte teacher I have hired to instruct you. Your aunt explained you had not had but a smattering of lessons with the instrument. As a duke's ward, we want you to have every advantage," the duchess replied.

"Oh!" Cat replied and turned, burying her head beneath the fluffy down pillow.

"This was a guest room, but I have commissioned new interiors for you and your sister. I think a nice, bright yellow, would be a pleasant color," the duchess continued.

"Meow," came a sound beneath the covers.

Cat shot back up in her bed.

"Was that a cat?" Her Grace asked.

"What would a cat be doing in my room?" asked Cat, extending her left hand down by her side.

"Indeed," replied her host. "Do you mind if I look?"

"A look?" Cat replied, innocence all over her face. What in the world would she say? Her sister would be furious. They had only been here a few days. Not even a week.

"Did His Grace return yesterday?" she asked, thinking he seemed to like her. Perhaps he would be an ally.

"Do not distract me," the duchess replied, reaching over, and pulling back the blue coverlet. A grey and white kitten emerged, stretching its front legs. And looking up at the woman.

"I suppose I should introduce you to Greyson," Cat inserted hopefully. "I realize what this must look like," she said, working her throat as if she was swallowing a worm. She desperately wanted the duchess to like Greyson. The other six kittens had been taken by the cook, who warned her to leave all seven with her, promising to feed them. Cat had fallen in love with this little one who seemed to walk on his white paws as if he was a prancing horse. So, she had ignored Mrs. Nettles' wise counsel.

"You brought a cat into the bedroom?" the duchess said, her voice rising.

"Well, it is really a kitten. I estimate him to be eight weeks, judging from his size," Cat answered, a bit too smartly. She realized it as soon as the last word left her mouth.

The duchess arched a brow and pulled the long velvet rope next to the bed. "Get dressed. I will see to the . . . kitten."

Cat noticed the kitten had disappeared. A moment later, they heard scratching and both she and the duchess turned their attention to the small box that Cat had used as the kitten's bed. In it, he had made a morning deposit. The smell reached them immediately. Neither said a word.

"I will get dressed immediately, Your Grace," Cat said. "Please let Greyson stay."

To her surprise, the older woman was still looking at the kitten, who had curled up on the floor outside of the box. "I am not pleased at all to discover this kitten in your room. However, you will find that I possess a heart. And I was once your age. I understand the need you have for a pet. I will speak to my son and see how he feels about this. It is his house, after all. In the meantime, clean this up before you come downstairs . . . yourself," she emphasized. "I will not have the servants responsible for the . . . excrements of your pet. And you should determine how best to train him."

"Thank you, Your Grace," Cat said, blushing.

"Yes. Well, I am still thinking about this, mind you. Be sure to rouse your sister and both of you be downstairs to break your fast within half-an-hour. Mr. Whitesides will be here at nine of the clock. I have never known the man to be late. She started to leave, but turned with a forced smile. "Heed what I say, Miss Stewart. I will not be made a fool of." With that, the woman left the room.

The door closed and Cat brought the kitten close to her chest and kissed it on the nose. "Your timing leaves much to be desired, Greyson. What were you thinking to be so bold as to show yourself to the duchess?" she clucked. She held the kitten out. "I cannot be upset with you. You are too sweet." Cat patted the animal and put him on her pillow, watching contentedly as he scratched the sheets relentlessly until he finally plopped down with a contented sigh.

She dashed to Beatrice's room next door and was relieved to find her sister already dressed. "The duchess requests our presence in the dining room. She has arranged pianoforte lessons at nine of the clock. And she discovered Greyson." She tried to put that last bit in quickly, hopefully unnoticed.

Beatrice stopped and grabbed Cat's arm, giving her a withering look. "Are you already making problems, Cat? Your manners would most unsettle Mama and Papa these past two days. We shall have nowhere to go but the orphanage if they turn us out. If not for Papa writing his solicitor of the duke's interest in looking after us, that would have been where we are—and there are no cats and kittens there."

"I cannot help that I love animals so much. You do, as well," Cat protested.

"And Aunt Esther warned us of this, as well. We cannot afford to be turned out," Beatrice repeated, obviously ignoring Cat's point.

"You are not a grown-up, Beatrice," pouted Cat, crossing her arms.

"I am old enough to marry. Had the flu not taken Mama, she would have introduced me to Society. I am six and ten," her older sister said.

"Fine. I will try to be . . . boring," agreed Cat. "It goes against my nature. And I believe the duke likes me."

"Do not count on it," replied Beatrice. "We have only been here a couple of days. Please control yourself. You are almost three and ten and know better, Cat."

"I know I am hungry and if I have to sit at a pianoforte and pretend to learn something that I have no interest in doing, I need to eat," Cat returned. "Can we go to the dining room now? I promise to behave."

"Yes." Beatrice grabbed her sister's hand and squeezed it. "I love you, Cat. I do not want us to be separated. I have heard all kinds of horror stories about orphanages."

Footsteps sounded from behind the girls. "I would never separate you girls," Lucas said, walking up to them. "Unless you make me miss my meal," he teased.

Cat shot her sister a look, as if to say, I told you he likes me. "Then you will never send us to an orphanage?" she pressed.

"That is not my plan," Lucas returned.

"Oh," Cat said quietly, noticing the duke did not say *never*. What if her sister was right? Perhaps she should speak to Cook before things got out of hand with the kittens.

"What do you say we break our fast together? My friends are probably already in the dining room," Lucas suggested.

Cat and her sister nodded. Cat squeezed her sister's hand, hoping to signal her that she would do as she suggested, after all.

That was a signal they used to cut through words. Her mother had always used it.

The thought of her mother filled her throat with a lump. Beatrice was right. They would not be happy with the way she had acted these last two days. For the life of her, Cat could not understand her behavior, either. Sometimes it seemed she got in trouble despite her best intentions.

"If your friends do not mind my sister and me joining you, Your Grace, we would love to," Beatrice said.

"Nonsense. You ladies are old enough to be included in most meals." He looked at Cat. "We shall endeavor to include you as much as possible."

"The duchess said we will have pianoforte lessons today, and I never like to play an instrument on an empty stomach," Cat put in. She would make the best of the lessons, too, even though she hated the pianoforte.

Canton Manor

HARRIETT WOKE ABRUPTLY when she heard talking in the hall outside of her door.

"Harriett, we have a visitor at the door, and he insists on seeing you personally." It was her father's voice. "Jane, is Harriett awake yet?"

"I am not sure, milord," Jane replied.

"Please see she gets up immediately."

Harriett moaned and sat up. She had entertained pretending to still be asleep, but it seemed that would not work. Whatever it was, her father was involved, and while her relationship with her father was still strained because of what he had done five years ago, she did not want to disappoint him—an old habit, to be sure.

"I am getting up, Father."

Jane scratched on the door and opened it. "My lady, you have a visitor."

"So I heard," Harriett said dryly, irritated at waking so early. She glanced outside the window. The sun must have just come up! Father's temperament illustrated the need to expedite the search for a home of her own. The only hesitation was deciding *where* she wanted to live. Her former husband's solicitor had written her a week past with listings of townhouses and other properties. She should have looked at them. It was hard to come back to live here once she had already been mistress of her own home. She sat up and moved her feet over the side of the bed, wiggling her feet into the warm slippers that were beneath her. "I am up." She realized her irritation showed through.

"I came as soon as I heard your father. The visitor banged on the door until Nichols opened it. He demanded to see you, your ladyship. Nichols woke your father's valet," Jane explained.

"Did he give his name? *Anything?*" Harriett felt a twinge of apprehension. Her late husband's cousin had inherited the title. He had insisted she move to the dowager house on the edge of the property and had little to do with her. She had spent the mourning period there. Recently, she had contacted the solicitor about the property she had gained from him in Bath and requested he sell it, determined to find a new place to live where Dudley had not lived. Her late husband's generosity toward her in his will had shocked her since he had been cruel and disparaging throughout their marriage. However, she had asked no questions.

"He will give no information except to ye, milady," Jane said. "He is tall, brawny, and has shoulder-length wiry hair. 'Tis is all I could see from my window in on the top floor."

Harriett did not know who that could be. Tremulously, she placed her housecoat about her and cinched it tightly. Jane brushed her hair into a semblance of style that would not embarrass her. Without another word, she left the room and joined her father, who was still waiting in the hall for her.

"Father, thank you for waiting for me. I confess, I cannot

fathom who this could be or about what it could be," she murmured.

"Certainly," he replied.

They moved to the parlor while Nichols opened the front door. "Her ladyship will see you," he said to the stranger. Nichols stepped aside and bade the man enter and go to the parlor. "May I have your name now, sir?"

"I am Mr. Jenkins," the man said, stepping inside.

Nichols showed him to the parlor and announced him to Lady Dudley.

"Lady Dudley, I have a missive for you from Lord William Dudley," Jenkins said, placing the missive in her hand. "Thank you for seeing me."

"Thank you, Mr. Jenkins." Harriett stood there and stared at the sealed vellum in her hand as Jenkins turned to leave. "I will open this in my room, Father."

"Of course," Scarsdale said. "I understand."

Back in her room, Harriett stared at the letter and finally broke the seal. She unfolded it and stared at the letter.

Dear Lady Dudley

We have important unfinished business. Let me know when it would be convenient for us to meet.

Regards,
Viscount William H. Dudley

Harriett read and reread the missive, committing it to memory. A shiver shot through her—one reminiscent of how Dudley made her feel. She had sworn to let no one make her feel that way again. Ever. There was no reason to meet with anyone from Dudley's family—it was the reason she left the dowager house. After what her dead husband had put her through, it was the last thing she wanted to do. She crumbled the letter and tossed it in the fireplace and wrapped her arms about her, reminding herself she was safe.

CHAPTER SEVEN

Two days later

L UCAS STOOD IN front of his stables, speaking with Mr. Benson,
his steward. Turning his attention to the structure itself, he
placed his hands on his hips and gazed upward. "I want this
expanded to provide more room for the grey and any more like
him I may gain," he said, gesturing with his left hand. "They
would be trained here, of course."

"Yes, Your Grace," Benson returned, scrawling on a small
tablet of folded papers he had with him. "Do you wish to have
the training rings enlarged, as well?"

"Of course. And add two. We should also expand the staff
with at least one more stablehand. I want Colton to stretch his
legs. I want a jockey working with him, almost daily."

His father, the late duke, had commissioned these stables
when he had inherited the title from his father. His father would
be happy with the addition of champion lineage and the expan-
sion of space, he reflected. "It is January. How much can be
accomplished before I head to London?"

"When do you plan to leave for London, Your Grace?" the
steward asked.

"Perhaps late March. I may have my mother and the young
ladies join me a few months later. My two wards need time to

grieve the loss of their parents. The timing could change," Lucas speculated, thinking through his plans as he adopted them. "Benson, have a few rooms added over the stables for the stablehands and on the bottom, add a few kennels for smaller animals, like dogs."

"As you wish, Your Grace." The man smiled. "I have had the architect who last worked on Pembley to sketch out the changes." Benson held out a large, rolled paper. "Perhaps we can roll these plans out to discuss in your study."

"A fine idea. I will meet you in there in twenty minutes," Lucas said. He glanced around the stables and called out to his ostler, who was mucking a stall. "Has something happened to the mother cat that was hanging around here—Whiskers, I believe we named her? I thought we might see her kittens." As a young boy, he had saved a small kitten and discovered he enjoyed having them around. He found them expert mousers, and they were normally gentle and calming companions for the horses. Many slept in the stalls with them.

The aging ostler, Mr. Franks, removed his hat and wrung it tightly in his hands. "Your Grace, a Miss Stewart, retrieved the mother cat and her kittens two days ago and suggested she would care for them."

"She did?" How curious. He wondered where they were being raised. "Which Miss Stewart? There are two," Lucas replied, amused.

"She introduced herself as Miss Cat Stewart," he answered, wiping his brow. "She was an engaging lass."

That sounded like Catherine, for certain. A smile curved his lips. She was going to be a handful. He had little experience with girls at that age. But Catherine was surely not the usual fare. "Did Miss Catherine mention the duchess when she removed the kittens?"

Lucas was very curious. His mother was a stickler for the animals being left in the stable area. While he was aware of his ability to make or break rules, he dared not cross his mother.

There had been a truce of sorts. She had promised not to bother him with marriage-minded ladies, and he allowed her to run the house as she saw fit—until and unless he married, of course. But he had no plans for that. Harriett's image flashed before him.

"No, Your Grace. However, a footman walked behind carrying the box of kittens."

"Thank you, Franks. I am sure the kittens were being seen to," Lucas returned. *What was that little hoyden up to, now?*

The ostler nodded and went back to mucking the stall. Miss Catherine Stewart was going to need a firm hand. *I wonder if Mother is up to the task.*

He and his brothers had certainly given Mother a challenge, but Father and the staff had been there to help. The realization he would truly have to help raise these young ladies washed over him and made him slightly queasy. Lucas turned and walked back toward the house, thrusting his hands in his pockets to warm them. Perhaps Cat thought the air too nippy for the small kittens. Whatever it was, he was certain she had justified it. And it will be amusing, he thought, snickering to himself.

Just as he approached the house, a loud racket in the kitchen area drew his attention and he turned toward it. The sound of clanging pots and pans, barks, and raised voices continued.

"What the . . .?" he said, opening the door.

The sight greeting him startled him. The cook sat sprawled on the floor, holding up a large basket of kittens to keep them away from the small black and white terrier that was trying to jump up to the rim of the basket. Six kitten faces of varying colors leaned over the edge of the basket, mewing down at the irritated dog. Two maids were trying to pick up the pots and pans, but were having a hard time holding on to them and dodging the irritated puppy at the same time.

"Shhh! Rascal, what are you doing inside the kitchen?" the cook asked.

The dog barked.

"Calm yourself," pleaded the cook, still holding the basket

high.

"Allow me to help you," Lucas said, lifting the basket of kittens from Mrs. Nettles. "Can you settle the dog down?" He nodded in the terrier's direction, still leaping up and trying to grab a kitten from the basket. The kittens, who could have escaped the basket on a whim, had curiously remained in the basket, taunting the dog from the wicker rim.

Lucas placed the basket on the worktable and helped his cook from the floor. Then he turned to the dog. *"Sit!"*

The dog immediately sat in front of the duke, trembling—and focusing its round, dark brown eyes and small pink and black nose on the tall man standing in front of him.

"Oh, Your Grace! She listened to you. How did you make her do that?" The older woman asked, clasping her hands.

"I told her to sit," he replied, resisting the urge to shake his head regarding the naivety of his cook. "What commands have you taught her?"

"I reckon I've taught her to eat, mostly. And go to the bathroom. Rascal has always been a cuddly one," Mrs. Nettles replied. "She usually never comes into the kitchen, Your Grace."

"Maybe keep up the sit command, holding your pointing finger toward her face, thus," he said, demonstrating.

"You always were a smart one, Your Grace," gushed the cook. Her face turned red.

"You are a dear lady, Mrs. Nettles," Lucas returned. "Have you met my two wards?"

The abruptness of his question seemed to have left her tongue-tied. She sputtered for a moment and finally, just nodded. "I met Miss Cat, yesterday. She asked me to find her a basket for some kittens." The cook hung her head, perhaps ashamed to have gone along with the young miss without asking for clarification. "A sweet young woman, Your Grace."

Lucas bit the inside of his mouth, fighting the impulse to smile. "May I ask how you wound up with the kittens in here?"

"I offered, Your Grace." The older woman stood straighter,

folded her hands, and looked up at Lucas. "I am truly sorry if I did something wrong."

"I am not upset with you, Mrs. Nettles. I simply want to find out what is going on . . . in the house." He gave a forced grin. It was apparent that young Miss Stewart was winning over the staff and making them coconspirators in her mischief. "Are these all the kittens? I thought there were seven." *Had one died already?*

"No, Your Grace. The young miss favored the grey and white," the cook replied.

Her explanation made sense. He would not be upset with his cook for doing as she was asked. Lucas laughed out loud. "Indeed! I think we have a young woman with a thirst for adventure. These kittens may need your tender care, Mrs. Nettles. To that end, you may help them, but . . ." he lowered his voice. "Unless there is an excellent reason to the contrary, I do not wish them in the house, and certainly not loose."

"Yes, Your Grace. The cook looked at the scullery maid. "Abby, help me set the rooms to rights. And return the kittens to the stable . . . in the basket. Leave a dish of milk with them. I will let Rascal out in the yard with a bowl of water." She looked up at Lucas.

"Thank you, Mrs. Nettles." On his way down the hall from the kitchen, he heard his mother's voice. She sounded out of sorts. He needed to sort all of this out with young Miss Stewart—before he found more pets in the house. His mother stopped short when she saw him leaving the kitchen area.

"Darling, what are you doing down here? I thought for sure you would be out in the stables working with that beautiful new pony you brought home."

His mother sounded as if she were discussing the weather, but it was obvious there was something amiss. "I might ask you the same, Mother." Lucas smiled easily at his mother. "You rarely come to the kitchen. Were you perhaps coming to pick out a kitten?"

She heaved a resigned sigh. "I was *not* coming to pick out a kitten. The younger Miss Stewart, Cat, has a big heart *and* a need for a pet. And has the kitten in her room."

"I see. Could you bring the girls to my study in half-an-hour, Mother?"

"We will be there, Lucas."

→≫≻×≺≪←

HARRIETT OPENED HER bedroom curtain and pulled back the drapes, enjoying the warmth of the sun. Taking a deep breath, she relaxed her shoulders, determined to enjoy herself. Glancing down at her ankle, she stretched her foot and tested it. It still hurt, but the pain was fading. Bearing down on it, she winced. Perhaps it would not be much longer.

A tap sounded at the door before Jane let herself into the room. "Milady, your sister asked that ye break yer fast with her," she said.

Harriett smiled to herself. Alice was never content to read a book. Her sister needed to be doing something all the time. It had been what she missed most about her sister. Alice was fun. "Then, let us not disappoint her, Jane."

"Will ye be going out, milady?" Jane inquired as she looked through Harriett's pressed dresses.

"I am not sure what Alice has in mind, but my foot is still quite sore. I would like to be out from under the doctor's orders. My plans are to remain about the house," Harriett said. "Perhaps I can talk my sister into painting with me. We could set up in the sunroom."

"That sounds like a good plan, milady," Jane said, as she helped her into her sapphire-blue, muslin morning dress.

"That sounds wonderful. I would try my new half-boots, but my ankle is still sore. I think the matching kid slippers might be better," Harriett said, turning to allow Jane to cinch her laces on her back.

Once Jane finished her hair, Harriett checked the mirror and pinched her cheeks. Accepting her cane from her maid's outstretched hand, Harriett nodded. "Thank you, Jane. I hope I will not need this much longer."

"It was kind of your sister to bring it to you," Jane acknowledged. "She has yer best interests at heart, I think."

"That is very generous of you. I know she can be a little . . . direct. I apologize for that," Harriett said, quietly.

"No need, milady. She has missed ye. I understand." Jane gave a quick smile before straightening the bedcovers.

"I hate to ask this of you, but would you see to Penelope for me? She will need a few minutes in the garden." Harriett hated to ask this of her maid.

"Be happy to, milady." The maid gently stroked the tiny kitten spread out on Harriett's pillow.

Harriett nodded. "Thank you. I realize she is not your responsibility, but I appreciate it. You said Alice is already downstairs waiting for me?"

"She is, ma'am," Jane returned.

"I will join her," she returned. She grabbed the cane and walked over to the puppy. "Be good Penelope. Do your business outside or Mother will never allow me to keep you indoors. And it is rather cold in the stables."

The puppy gave a soft bark, as if she understood.

A few minutes later, she walked into the dining room and heard her mother loudly whispering to her sister at the sideboard. "Have I intruded?" She placed her cane near the chair directly in front of the sideboard and pivoted to get some food.

Her mother's face paled, a certain sign she had been the subject.

"It sounded like an important conversation. Do you plan to enlighten me?" *When had she become so direct with people?* She knew the answer. It was when she was dutifully married off to a man that had no business being married, without explanation. She realized she was still irritated with her parents—*both of them.*

Alice winced slightly, looking *caught*. "Mother and I were discussing some errands. She plans to go to the town to have a new pelisse, and some hats made. I was suggesting we join her. Your brown pelisse could be the one you had when you married. Did the man never buy you new clothes?" Realizing her faux pax, Alice added, "I would like to order a wine-colored one, as well. I like the cranberry color with my hair."

Leave it to Alice to dredge up the past—something that could never be changed and only reminded her of the hole in her heart. She had resigned herself to never knowing the love a man could have for a woman. Dudley had never loved her. "I would have had to wait longer for a pelisse, and I wished to leave as soon as I could. Perhaps Mother could pick out fabric and have one made for me," Harriett finally answered, irritated. She glared at her sister, feeling peevish. "And I do not feel up to walking." She pointed toward the cane.

Alice gave her a quick smile. "I thought we could make it a mother-daughter excursion, like we used to do. We could have the coach follow us along the walk as we move from building to building, in case you tire."

The thought unexpectedly appealed to Harriett. "That would be lovely, Alice, and if the coach stayed close, it might work for me." She shook her head. "I apologize to the both of you. I heard the whispers and after the many conversations about . . . well, never mind. I am sorry. This will be fun. Perhaps I can pick up a toy for Penelope." Her sister noticeably winced . . . *again*. "I see. You have not mentioned the puppy to Mother."

"No darling, I was just getting around to that when you appeared."

"Girls . . . I mean, ladies. Sorry, that is an old habit. I already know about the puppy, and it is fine. I expect the dog could not have found a better person to be a companion to," her mother said.

The word *companion* stung, although Harriett knew her mother had meant no harm by it. "Thank you, Mother," Harriett said, as she filled her plate. She had the distinct impression that there was still something going on here that she was not privy to and determined to watch and listen. Mother had agreed too readily to having a dog in the house.

"Yes, thank you, Mother. I meant to say something. If I had a half-penny for each of my good intentions . . ." Alice said, letting the sentence drift off with a smile.

"Yes, dear," Mother finished, ladling some pan-fried potatoes onto her plate. "The road is paved with good intentions."

The ladies took their seats, and a footman came around with their hot tea. "Thank you, Timmons. I realized I forgot the bacon. Would you be so kind as to put two pieces on my plate?"

"Of course, my lady," the footman answered, hurrying to do her bidding.

The bacon smelled delicious.

They ate in silence for a while. Harriett had not realized how hungry she had gotten. "What time do you plan to leave for town, Mother?"

"This has been lovely," Mother said, wiping her mouth with a serviette and taking a last sip of tea. "Would you ladies be ready in a half-hour?" Her mother stood to leave. "I will have Nichols send for the carriage."

"That is perfect for me," Alice said, also finishing her morning meal and standing. "I will grab my reticule from upstairs."

"Would you be so kind as to get mine also? That will keep me from having to go back upstairs," Harriett asked.

Harriett watched her sister and her mother walk upstairs together and could not miss the conspiratorial whispers when they thought they had moved beyond her hearing. *What are they up to?*

CHAPTER EIGHT

"Have a seat, ladies," Lucas demanded, gesturing for the girls to take a seat in front of his desk. He had chosen his study because it offered the more imposing backdrop for this conversation. His mother quietly took a seat off to the right of his desk, leaving the seats directly in front of the duke for the girls.

"I am glad to see you are settling into Pembley Manor, Beatrice and Cat." Lucas purposely looked at each. "However, we have rules here. I realize you have been here a matter of days, but our rules are not such that a reasonable person would not know them—without being told." He looked at Cat and the girl merely smiled at him. "As an example, we have a stable cat—Whiskers—that we have been taking care of for several years. She recently had seven kittens. Yet, when I checked on her today, she and her kittens were missing. He looked at Cat again. "Cat, you brought those kittens into the house. Where did you leave Whiskers?"

"The kittens are safe, Your Grace," Cat assured him.

"The mother cat. Where is she?" he persisted.

"I left her in the stable. I promise," Cat replied.

He looked at the young girl. "I may not explain this adequately to you," he said, looking at his mother for help—any help. "But you separated the mother cat from her kittens . . . all the kittens, and they are her babies. She left the stable to look for them."

Beatrice stirred in her seat before turning to her sister. "Cat, how could you have left the mother without her kittens? And how could you have bothered the kittens?" she hissed. "Mother told you many times you have to leave the babies with the mother. You cannot separate the mother from her babies."

So, this type of thing had occurred before. The mischief miss had not learned her lesson. "Apparently, I will have to make one of our rules known to you, Cat. The kittens stay with their mother, in the stable. They are bonded, and I have no plans to separate any of them. The stable needs mousers, and the horses like the cats."

"Are there other cats?" she asked innocently.

"There are a few." He glanced at his mother. "They were probably in the different stalls with the horses, sleeping. As I consider it, perhaps they were hiding." Lucas smiled at the precocious young woman. "There is a friendship of sorts between the cats and the horses that is advantageous to both, and I want to leave it in place."

"That is unusual, is it not, Your Grace?" asked Beatrice, who had leaned forward, thrilled to learn about the horses and the cats.

"I suppose," Lucas admitted. "I have my theory."

"Could you share it?" Beatrice asked. "I mean no disrespect, Your Grace. However, I am very curious."

"I understand, Beatrice." Lucas smiled. "I had never experienced it until I found an injured kitten as a child. Our stablehand knew some animal medicine and kept the kitten in the barn. A day or two later, I found him cuddled up next to a horse. My thinking is it has something to do with the calmness of the horses and the curiosity of the cats. The cats sleep next to them in the stalls. The cats do not present any kind of threat to the horse, and the horse enjoys the companionship."

"The horses would not hurt the kittens?" Cat asked.

"No, they would not," the duchess put in. "I had not believed it until I saw it myself. However, if you want to have the kitten, perhaps the duke can work something out for you."

Lucas turned back to Cat. "You have the little grey one with white feet?"

She nodded.

"That should be fine, but while he is so small, bring him to be with his mother for a few more weeks. Once he is about three months old, maybe we can wean him from his mother."

"The cats also keep the mice out of the horse feed," Cat added.

"That's right!" Lucas laughed.

"I apologize for acting without asking, Your Grace," Cat said. "Greyson will enjoy seeing his mother. I will bring him for visits every day."

"That was not what I said to do, but it is progress," Lucas smiled and glanced at his mother, who was also smiling. "Cat, you need to live within the rules of the house. Is that understood?"

"Yes," she said, nodding. "I will endeavor to do better."

"Good. I believe we are done here," the duchess said. "But do not leave." She turned to Lucas. "I plan to take the girls to town. I thought a visit to the haberdashery might be in order. If they must wear mourning colors, we can at least give them pretty hats. I do not believe that would be disrespectful to the dead."

"I agree, Mother. Are you going today?" Lucas asked.

"Yes. The coach should be outside now," his mother replied.

"Ladies . . . do not let me stand in your way!" Lucas stood.

"When we get back, we have pianoforte lessons," the duchess said, as she stood and headed toward the door. "Mr. Whitesides will be here this afternoon, shortly after we return."

An audible sigh escaped Cat. "May I have permission to get my reticule? Beatrice, I can get yours as well."

"Certainly, Miss Catherine," his mother said. "We have a tight schedule. Be quick."

"Yes, Your Grace," Cat replied.

Fifteen minutes later, Lucas saw Cat pass the door to his study on her way to the front of the house. Curious, he stepped from behind his desk and quietly stepped into the hall, ready to assist.

"Where is your reticule?" he heard his mother ask. His mother had waited for the girl in the anteroom. He could imagine her frustration.

"Oh!" Cat looked at her and gave a sheepish look. "I wanted to say goodbye to Greyson! He is so adorable and was sleeping on my pillow, purring away. It was hard to leave him."

He walked out towards the door and helped them with their pelisses. "It looks to be an excellent day for a jaunt to town, Mother," Lucas said, nodding toward the door. "I have some books to go over but am hard-pressed not to visit my new colt and try to work with him."

"Why do you not do that, dear?" his mother said, grabbing her muff. She turned to the girls. "I have noticed neither of you have muffs. We will need them. Being this close to the sea, we get wetter, winter weather. A muff is wonderful for those long carriage rides."

Lucas looked at Cat. There was a curious look of smugness about her. *What had she really been up to, upstairs?* At first, he thought Beatrice would be the reason to have a governess— someone to relieve his responsibilities with a coming out, and of course, to teach the younger sibling. But he was beginning to see things a lot differently. His younger ward was someone to watch. Perhaps he would look for advice on a school for young girls— that bore thinking about. He did not want the child to think she was not wanted. It was not a situation he relished, but he had made the promise and would keep it.

"Egerton," he said, walking past the butler's small office behind the parlor. He watched the man almost knock over his chair to stand when he saw his employer. Lucas made a mental note to summon Egerton in a more traditional fashion and save the poor man from this again. "Egerton, I have been thinking about the two young ladies and have decided to see my solicitor about them." He handed his butler a sealed letter. "Please have a footman frank it for me today. I would like to see Mr. Innes on his next visit to Richmond."

"Yes, Your Grace." The older man looked up at him. "Is there a problem?"

Normally, this was not a question the older man would have ever asked. However, Lucas detected a fondness for the girls from Egerton, particularly for Cat. She seemed to have won over his staff. And if indicators from the kitchen kitten debacle, as he was now referring to it in his mind, were any sign, Cat had wormed her way into their good graces and was using them as co-conspirators in her shenanigans. His gut told him there would be much more. "No, not exactly. I merely want to discuss provisions for them, in the event of . . ." He let the sentence drop. "Was that Trask I saw accompanying my mother on her trip to town?"

"Yes, it was, Your Grace. And please forgive my forwardness. I have grown fond of the two of them—especially the younger one. She seems . . . a lot like you were in your youth. I expect she will keep us on our toes," he said with an uncharacteristically broad grin. "Yes, indeed."

"I suspect you have the right of it. You are a shrewd judge of character, Egerton," Lucas replied, smiling fondly at the man who had been more than a butler to him growing up. "You helped me out of a scrape or two as a young boy. I suspect we are in for a few dust-ups with young Miss Stewart."

Smiling, the aging man nodded. "Yes, Your Grace. I suspect we are."

His mother could handle this, he mused, as he headed back to his study.

"LADIES, THE MILLINER is on the right. Let us stop there, first." The duchess banged on the ceiling with her cane, before setting the stick beside her. She only brought it with her when she was in her coach or when in London. The coach stopped, and the footman helped them down. "Thank you, Trask."

The footman nodded. "Shall I accompany you, Your Grace?"

"I have nothing to pick up yet. I am merely placing orders. We shall go to the modiste's next."

He inclined his head. "I will remain here, should you need me, Your Grace."

A small bell rang as the shop door closed behind the three ladies.

"Welcome, Your Grace. What can I do for you today?" A small round woman with thinning grey hair scurried around the counter to meet her. The duchess stepped back to avoid a collision. "Mrs. Toppin, my I introduce to you the newest additions to our family? His Grace has become guardian to Miss Beatrice Stewart and Miss Catherine Stewart." Both girls took a tiny step forward as she called their names—obviously they had been taught that, she mused.

"Pleased to meet you," they said together.

The duchess smiled. Perhaps she was making some headway. She had doubted it this morning when Lucas uncovered the kittens in the kitchen, of all places. With the terrier. She would address that with Mrs. Nettles. The old woman was the salt of the earth. She could never hurt her feelings. "Miss Beatrice and Miss Catherine will need hats, gloves, and muffs. I also plan to commission pelisses for the girls, and one more for myself, so we will need the hats and gloves to match. The girls have lost their parents and will be in mourning, so I would like a little color to their hats."

"What a wonderful idea, Your Grace. You are most forward-thinking. If the girls would let me know the style of hats they prefer and perhaps some colors they favor, we will get to work on them," the milliner replied.

"That will be lovely. Are you still working with Mrs. Thimblesby, the seamstress next door? Winter is upon us, after all. While a trip to London might sound wonderful, it can be avoided because of your wonderful services here. I thought to have several things made."

The older woman gushed, clearly pleased with the business she was about to earn. "Certainly, Your Grace. I have a new helper who can come out and take the necessary measurements for the hats. Do you require shawls? I have a lovely new shipment of shawls and other fripperies over here." Mrs. Toppin pointed to the area of the store she had come from, only moments before, highlighting a counter display of shawls and ribbons.

"Yes! After we place the order for the hats, we shall look through them. Ladies, what colors do you favor?"

The girls gave the woman what she needed.

"Please send word when they are finished, and we will send Trask to collect them," the duchess said, as she ushered the girls out the door.

As they approached the next shop, she thought she recognized the ladies entering ahead of her. "Lady Dudley and Lady Penfield. How delightful to see you both this morning!" The duchess made introductions to her two charges. "His Grace has become guardian, and with their arrival this past week, we are making sure they have everything they need to get through our chilly winters."

"Indeed, Your Grace," Lady Alice Penfield agreed. "It is wonderful to see you. You look the picture of eternal youth, as usual," she remarked.

"Oh! Thank you! You are generous," the duchess replied. She tried to keep up her appearance, but since her husband's death, it had been hard to be motivated. However, these girls seemed to be just the jolt she required. It was wonderful to feel needed again. She would do her best to help her son. And she had already begun to think of the best way to help him. Lady Harriett Dudley.

"Ladies, I have not raised girls, and I feel a little out of my depth here. I wonder if you might have a few minutes to help us select some appropriate materials for dresses for the girls. They are in mourning, but I do not want them to feel they are imprisoned, if you catch my meaning." She felt comfortable speaking her mind with the Scarsdale women. They could never be considered passive in their thoughts, she mused, smiling.

"How lovely of you to say," exclaimed Lady Penfield. "I would be most happy to help."

The duchess saw her motion to Lady Dudley, who, she just noticed, was using a cane. "His Grace told me about your horse accident," she said solicitously. "How is your ankle?"

Lady Dudley blushed. "It is much better. I am trying to do as the doctor said, but my sister, here, never stays still. I am quite sure she will have me running by the end of the week," she replied with a laugh.

Lady Penfield snorted. "I would have that if I could. But I am afraid Mother would find a problem with ladies running about."

"Miss Catherine, I would be most happy to help you and your sister select some suitable materials for a coat," Lady Dudley offered.

Pleased, the duchess watched the three of them move toward a table with woolen coat materials before turning to Lady Penfield. "I would like a word, if you would not mind," she said, quietly.

Lady Penfield nodded, and the two women quietly edged toward some fabric on the opposite wall. "I need to find some suitable materials for their mourning gowns. Poor girls are using their older gowns dyed black. I want them to have some newer ones that fit properly," she said in a quiet voice, conscious that the seamstress had also followed Lady Dudley and the girls to the other side of the room. "I think you can be of help to me," she said in a whisper, and then looked up to make sure they were not overheard.

"It sounds conspiratorial," Lady Penfield returned with a wink. "I am all ears!"

The duchess glanced up at Lady Dudley's sister. This could be easier than she thought. "How long will you be here in our fine county?" she asked, running some delicate muslin fabric through her fingers.

"I will be here as long as my sister needs me. My husband is most understanding. I could not leave her in her present state . . . injured . . ."

". . . and unmarried," the duchess boldly asserted, deciding to see if her instincts were right.

"Correct!" Lady Penfield replied. "That is a lovely fabric. If Mrs. Thimblesby has it in some more flattering shades of lavender, the grey ones, of course, it might be perfect for the next few months of mourning for the young ladies."

"I quite agree. May I be so bold as to ask if our quiet tones could mean we may be of the same mind on a certain issue?" the duchess ventured.

"Of course! I am even more certain that we have the same end in mind. How can I help?" Lady Penfield replied.

"We are looking for a governess. I feel I can hold that employment off if I can secure valuable assistance in certain areas that could help me guide the young ladies while we are conducting a search for a governess. If you feel your sister might offer me advice on the girls, I feel her presence at the manor would be a boon to our mutual desire to see them get back together," Her Grace asserted boldly, in hushed tones.

Lady Penfield smiled. "My sister is wonderful at painting and might help with some divertive activities on that front. What do you think?"

"I think we will make a wonderful team! Let us conclude this conversation. Perhaps you can stop by tomorrow and we can discuss this a little more," the duchess suggested.

"How would mid-morning sound? I should give my sister some time to relax and heal," Lady Penfield replied with a wink.

"Scandalous!" the duchess said with a snicker. "I have never engaged in this type of thing with my son before. However, while I struggle with a small amount of guilt, what they say about desperate times is true. A boost in the right direction is called for, and I do not wish to waste the opportunity, while your sister is here, in town." She looked toward Lady Dudley and the girls and felt pleased to see their heads together over some fabric. They had paid no attention to her or Lady Penfield's presence.

"I should warn you," Lady Penfield whispered. "It may prove harder than you think. My sister staked out that she never plans to marry again. The first husband was . . . less than desirable for her."

The duchess nodded. She looked over towards Mrs. Thimblesby. "This would be a lovely fabric for some dresses for the girls, when you have a minute."

"I will look forward to seeing you tomorrow. We can determine the best way to reach out to Harriett."

"Splendid idea," the duchess agreed as they walked up behind the other group. "I love that fabric for you, Cat, dear," she said, approving of the lighter burgundy wool the girl was holding.

"Goodness! I have completely monopolized your time, Lady Dudley! The girls seemed to appreciate your commentary on the fabrics, I forgot you must have had ideas for your own dressmaking needs," the duchess gushed.

"Nonsense. It was my pleasure, Your Grace," Lady Dudley replied. "My sister decided we need new pelisses and accoutrements—hence the reason for our outing. The fabric that Miss Catherine picked out is lovely. So as not to match too much, I shall go a shade or two deeper."

The younger girl smiled, clearly pleased with what Lady Dudley had said, which thrilled the duchess. It was not necessary, but would clearly be a boon to her plans if the girls liked Lady Dudley.

"I look forward to seeing you ladies again . . . soon," the duchess said.

"And we, as well, ladies," Lady Penfield acknowledged.

As Trask helped them into the coach, Cat leaned forward and waved to the two ladies that had come to the door of the shop to say goodbye. "I like Lady Dudley very much."

CHAPTER NINE

Later that day

A S THEY ARRIVED home, the duchess noticed the small buggy that the pianoforte teacher used parked on the sunny side of the drive, with the horse getting water from a small trough that had been placed for it nearby. She wondered how the lesson would go. The last one had been a near disaster. Cat had been most uncooperative, claiming she did not know her scales, and they needed to start there. The duchess suspected the young girl of duplicity and wondered why. She did not miss the surprised look her sister had given, but unless one of them gave better information, there was a limited way for her to know otherwise. It would place them further behind where they needed to be on the instrument at this age.

A niggling feeling urged her to pay close attention to the girl. When they were in the music room, she pressed the younger sibling a bit more. "Cat, my dear. I wonder if you can go first on the pianoforte. I had it tuned after your first lesson, so your scales should be even prettier to hear.

Cat gave a noticeable gulp. "I am not ready, Your Grace."

"Have you practiced, my dear?" the duchess persisted.

"I . . . well . . . not exactly," the younger girl grimaced. "I have not had time."

"Really?" the duchess replied in exasperation before she could check herself. She had not meant to embarrass either girl. Raising boys, she decided then, had been easier. One expected younger boys to shade the truth in favor of mischief.

"That is disappointing," Mr. Whitesides said, in a disapproving tone, possibly realizing he would have to step up his classroom discipline. Withdrawing a small silver box from his waistcoat pocket, he extracted a pinch of snuff. Sniffing the item into his nostril, he breathed in slowly before exhaling. His ritual complete, he turned to the two girls. "Miss Beatrice, may we hear the piece you have been practicing?"

Beatrice took a seat behind the instrument and gave her sister a curious glance. "Would you accompany me, sister? This is a song you know well."

She knows the song, but not her scales. How odd, the duchess noted.

"I . . ." Cat stuttered her reply, but after glancing in the duchess's direction, decided. "Yes! That could be fun." She strode up to the seat and helped find the song for her sister. "Ready," she said, offering a bright smile.

As her sister played, the pianoforte music sounded completely wrong. The notes were wrong, muffled at times, and nonexistent at others. Mr. Whitesides jumped up and went to the pianoforte. "The duchess just had this instrument tuned. Perhaps you need to press the keys a little more strongly. Every keyboard has its unique touch," he encouraged.

Again, Beatrice started playing and Cat sang the words. It sounded horrendous to the duchess's ears. It was not so much the singing, but the playing. Had Beatrice not practiced?

Beatrice, however, kept playing and looking at her sister with what looked like a forced smile. The duchess did not know Beatrice that well, yet, but this had all the earmarks of some scrapes she and her own sister had seen growing up. Something was going on here.

"Can we stop, ladies?" Mr. Whitesides said, interrupting.

"Your Grace, if you will permit me saying, perhaps we should have the instrument re-tuned."

"May I?" Lucas said, walking into the room. "I have been listening at the door and did not wish to disturb, but the sounds coming from the pianoforte reminded me of something I learned in school." He walked up to the instrument and smiled at his charges.

"Certainly, Your Grace," Mr. Whitesides said, and nervously indicated the two ladies should get off the seat at once, clearing the way for Lucas.

"My son enjoyed learning the pianoforte. It might be lovely to one day have one or both of the girls accompany him," interjected his mother in a befuddled tone. "He does not sing," she said with a distracted tone, curious what was going on.

"I do not know if the girls would appreciate my interfering with their lessons, and you are right. I cannot sing," he said. He lifted a small candelabra from the top of the pianoforte and placed it on the floor nearby. Then, taking the edge of the top of the pianoforte, he lifted it carefully.

"Perhaps we should have the piano tuned," he said, closing it. "Mother, maybe Mr. Whitesides should issue his lessons to the girls, and we can call it a day on the instruction for today."

"Why certainly." She dismissed the teacher and then walked up to her son. "What did you find?"

When the teacher left the room, he called the girls back. "Perhaps you ladies could give me a hand, here."

The girls looked at each other and walked toward the pianoforte and he noticed the reticence in both. He had a suspicion of what had occurred. Once they stood at the pianoforte, the duke lifted the lid. A light lavender ribbon-like fabric wrapped around several of the chords.

Beatrice glanced toward her sister but said nothing.

CAUGHT! DRAT IT. Perhaps she had acted too impulsively with this prank. Cat's only thought was getting out of playing the insipid instrument. Never had she stopped to gauge the consequences of such an action. The duke did not look pleased, and she suspected from his expression, he knew her culpability. She dared not look at Beatrice but could feel the glare of her anger. If they were thrown out of this home, she would be to blame. They would have nowhere to go but an orphanage, Aunt Esther had said, telling them her home was too small for children of any age. She could tell them why she had done it, but it would make the duchess angry, and she needed *at least* one ally. The duchess had been very understanding with Greyson.

"My goodness, Lucas! How in the world did those . . . ?" The duchess stopped talking and reached into the chords and pulled off one of the ribbons. It was one of the ribbons they purchased earlier this week.

Uh-oh! Cat thought. The ribbon was one of the new ones they had bought to match the pelisse fabric and from the look on her face, Cat knew the duchess recognized it.

"Mother, do you have any thoughts on this matter?" Lucas asked, giving his mother a knowing look.

"Son, I believe we have a prankster in our midst. It seems we will need to reform the mischief-maker, much like your father and I reformed you."

"*Reform* is a strong word, Mother." He snickered. "I assure you; I appreciate a well-executed prank. However," Lucas said, looking at Cat, "sometimes, better judgment and a longer stretch of timing between tomfooleries gives intended victims an opportunity to better appreciate the joke. But when the mischief is continual, it has the opposite effect."

"Yes. What do you suggest, Your Grace?" his mother said, seeming to agree with her son.

"First, we need to determine the culprit. Does anyone want to confess?" Lucas asked.

Silence prevailed. It did not surprise Cat her sister held her tongue. Bea was not a tattler, but Cat knew she would receive a tongue-lashing when they were alone. It was up to Cat to confess. She opened her mouth to say something and closed it.

"Yes, Cat. Were you about to say something?" the duchess asked.

"No, ma'am. I was merely going to say it looked a waste of a very good ribbon."

"Indeed!" the older woman intoned, with an astonished look on her face.

Cat needed to confess—she wanted to confess. But her heart beat furiously from fear and she held back.

"I did it," Beatrice said, stepping forward. "And I apologize."

"I am shocked to hear this," the duchess said, looking in Cat's direction with a withering look.

She knows. Again, Cat tried to speak up, but nothing came out.

"Why would you do such a thing, Beatrice?" Lucas asked. He glanced at Cat before looking back to her sister.

"I had not practiced and was afraid to embarrass myself . . ." she started saying before Cat cut her off.

"I did it," Cat managed. "I am truly sorry. My sister had nothing to do with this. Please do not send us to the orphanage. If you must send someone, send me. Bea needs a launch into Society. It was what Mama wanted for her. She deserves a coming out. It was me, and I am the one who should be punished."

The long moment of silence that ensued was as difficult as any punishment could have been. If only she had confessed immediately, she chastised herself. Now, Bea had stepped up and the whole mess had gotten complicated—a *real muddle*, Mama would call it. Thoughts of her mother immediately saddened her. She would not have been proud of Cat for this. *What had she been thinking?* Her lower lip quivered, and she had begun to tremble, something she could not recall doing since she had been a small girl.

"We are not sending either of you to an orphanage. I thought

I made that clear," Lucas finally said. "Why did you do it, Cat?"

Had she been two, she could have run from the room. But she was not two. She was almost three and ten. "I dislike playing the pianoforte," she said simply, looking up at the duke and holding both hands together to calm herself.

"Ah. I see. Well, what *do* you enjoy?" he persisted, his tone not as stern.

Nothing, really, she thought. *Nothing they will let me do.* She liked to ride astride on her horse, fish with her father, whom she missed more and more every day, and in the warm weather, she enjoyed swimming. Beatrice enjoyed the frillier activities like singing, playing the pianoforte, and sewing.

"I like to paint," she offered. Now that she thought about it, she enjoyed painting, if she could be allowed to paint animals like squirrels and birds.

Lucas reached into the pianoforte and untwisted the remaining ribbon from around the chords. "Painting, huh? How about you, Beatrice? Do you enjoy the pianoforte?"

"I do, Your Grace. Please do not be hard on my sister. This has all been a change—losing Mama and Papa and coming here." A fat tear rolled down the girl's cheek. "We both miss them terribly." She looked at Cat. "Mama always thought frustration made Cat act out more."

Lucas took his thumb and wiped the tear from her cheek. "There will be no punishment . . . not this time." He narrowed his eyes at Cat. "But I expect an apology to the others involved in this, young lady."

"I will, Your Grace. I will pen an apology note to Mr. Whitesides immediately." Even though she found it hard to like a man that pinched his nose before speaking to her. She looked at his mother. "Your Grace, I apologize for my trouble. I truly do. I meant only to get out of the lesson and did not think my actions through."

His mother smiled. "We were all young, Cat. I think you can be forgiven."

Cat hugged her sister. "I am sorry Bea. I should have spoken up before you did. You are the best of sisters."

Bea wiped a rogue tear away and smiled at Cat. "You are also the best of sisters."

"Mother wants the two of you to be happy, as do I. If you will let us know what activities you prefer, we will do our best to accommodate—within reason," the duke said.

I should not mention riding astride, for now, she thought.

"It has been quite an eventful day, girls. Dinner will be served soon. Mrs. Nettles has promised a surprise. Perhaps a respite for both of you, before changing for dinner, would be suitable," the duchess suggested.

⇒⟫⟪⇐

As THE YOUNG ladies departed for their rooms, Lucas turned to his mother. "Cat needs a firm hand. I will do my best to find a suitable governess as quickly as possible, Mother."

"Yes . . . and she reminds me a lot of you, Lucas. Despite the trouble, you seemed unflappable. Perhaps the right guidance will help direct her energies," the duchess murmured.

"You have that look about you, Mother. The one that says you are up to something," Lucas said cautiously. A look flickered across his mother's face before she schooled her features. It was just a flash, but he saw it.

"Nonsense! Why would you say such a thing?" his mother questioned in a pained voice.

Lucas started to say otherwise, but decided it was better not to. "As soon as we secure suitable candidates for governess, I will seek your opinion."

"That is all I can ask . . . for the children," his mother emphasized. "We must be careful and hire the right governess." She paused. "It could take time. What would you think of my bringing in some tutors . . . dancing, painting, and some skills the girls need to gain and polish so we will not lose time?"

"You have leave to employ who you need, Mother," he relented.

"Thank you, Son," she said, beaming.

As Lucas watched his mother leave, suspicion took root in his gut. The woman seemed to smile much more broadly over what he had offered, than seemed normal, and it gave him pause. He had the distinct feeling more mischief was afoot, but not from Cat.

CHAPTER TEN

A few days later

"**Y**OUR GRACE, YOU have a visitor," Egerton said, stepping inside the mahogany-paneled breakfast room.

Both the duke and his mother looked up from their morning meal.

"I apologize, Your Graces," Egerton said, appearing flustered. "The visitor wishes to see *Her* Grace." The duchess accepted the proffered card.

"Thank you, Egerton. Please show her to the parlor. I will be there shortly." The duchess took a hurried sip of her hot tea and dabbed at her lips. "Mrs. Nettles has outdone herself with these sweet rolls. Please bring tea and more of these sweet rolls to my parlor for my guest."

"Yes, Your Grace." The footman gave a half bow and departed the room.

"Anyone special, Mother?" He nodded toward the tray of the treat. "You are offering your favorite sweet," he observed with a sly grin.

"Yes, I am," she returned with a warm smile. "As hard as it shall be, I will refrain from taking a second." She lightly touched her stomach, drawing attention to the small waistline she still maintained. "However, I thought my guest might enjoy it." The duchess glanced about the empty room and stood. On impulse, she walked up to him and gave him a hug.

"What was that for?" he asked.

"Nothing special. It has been too long since I have shown you any affection, son. Sometimes I just feel the need to hug my son. You rarely stay still long enough for one." She nodded toward the tray of buns. "I will leave them for you and your friends, who," she arched a brow and gave a soft laugh, "are usually up before you are."

"We were up late playing cards and shooting billiards, Mother."

"You owe me no explanation. I enjoy having them here. It feels like old times." She stopped at the door and looked back at him. "*Good old times.* Time moves too quickly," she added before leaving the room.

It had not escaped his notice that Mother never mentioned whom she was meeting. Added to that, she sent some of Mrs. Nettles' infamous buns to her parlor instead of the usual fare of biscuits. Had she not done that, he may never have given it a thought. There must be a sense of familiarity to the person, because the buns were messy and could not be eaten neatly in front of company. He felt guilty for his suspicious nature, but curious all the same—and could not shake either.

Before he could dwell on it more, the door opened and Clarendon and Romney sauntered into the room, laughing over some inane comment one had made. Noticing Lucas sitting there, Romney smiled. "I could have closed my eyes and followed that delicious scent into this room. Are those Chelsea buns?" Romney asked. "My parents frequently indulged us and had them brought to the townhouse when we were in town."

"No. Well, maybe," Lucas amended. "They are Mrs. Nettles' variety. She learned to make them years ago and has been spoiling my family for a generation. I have had both and these are the clear winners," he drawled.

Romney moseyed over to the tray of buns. "I cannot imagine . . .," he started as he stuffed a bun unceremoniously into his mouth, ". . . anything . . . oh wow! These are delicious." He licked his lips to clear the wet sugary concoction from around his mouth. "I declare these Nettles buns superior. They melt in your mouth!"

"Yes, quite right," Lucas agreed, reaching for one himself.

"Should I have one before I help myself to the food?" Clarendon mused.

"I encourage you to fill your plate first, or you will fill up on these. They are decadent," Lucas replied.

"Quite right, my friend," Romney added, filling up a plate and taking his seat. "What is on the agenda for today? I look forward to checking out your new colt. If his bloodlines are even half an indication, I would wager he is a great addition to your stable."

"I had hoped we could do that today. My stablehands have been working with him, but I have looked forward to the three of us putting him through his paces," Lucas said, wiping his hands. Getting up, he picked up some small bowls and poured water from a pitcher into each one. "These fingerbowls are a requirement for us when we eat these," he laughed.

"Thank you," both men said together, simultaneously reaching for a bowl.

"I like the name Colton. Are you firm with the name change?" asked Clarendon, wiping his hands dry. "I want to know where to place my money."

Lucas smirked at his friend. "Yes. His old name was Colton, and I thought about keeping that one, but perhaps it would be better luck to rename him, and I like the name, Colton," he replied.

"I am not the superstitious type. However, I am observant. I meant to mention," Clarendon began. "I heard voices as I was getting dressed to come downstairs. It is not my business, but I suppose my curious nature got the better of me. I looked out the window and saw Lady Penfield arrive—at least she looked like Lady Dudley's sister. I thought to mention it to you in case you wanted to escape."

Lucas started. "Lady Penfield," he murmured. Although he tried to ignore it, that niggling feeling had returned. "I believe she is visiting Mother . . ." His sentence dropped off as he recalled his last conversation with his mother. *She is up to something.* He just did not know what, but intended to find out. "Perhaps my mother has some sort of charity involvement beginning and hopes to ensnare the good Lady Penfield's efforts on its behalf."

"Perhaps she plans an extended stay in Richmond," Clarendon agreed.

"She is probably here to visit her sister," Lucas replied absently. Somehow, this had to do with his mother, but he was not sure of the connection. He did not recall his mother being friendly with Harriett's sister. His mother had never engaged in marriage machinations for her sons. Manipulation had never been her style—but direct assault? Now that could be another thing entirely. Guilt gnawed at him. How was it reasonable to expect her to never want grandchildren? Lucas struggled with his thoughts, particularly guilt for thinking the worst of Mother's motives. Yet, a voice inside persisted—*she had never mentioned a friendship with Harriett's sister before.*

"I am ready to see the colt if you are. Colton has had a few days to rest since arriving here," he said, standing, ready to change the subject. "Our horses are being saddled and brought to the front. I thought we could ride out to the back stables after breakfast."

"Good idea." Romney patted his belly. "I may have overdone it with the buns," he said, giving the three men a hearty laugh. "It would not do for me to have those every morning."

The three men hoisted themselves into their saddles and rode off towards the stable area. When they arrived, they noticed the grey being walked around the ring, outside.

Lucas slid from his saddle and handed the reins to the waiting stablehand. "How is he doing?" he said, nodding in the grey's direction. "I would like to ride him," he added.

"Yer 'orse is a fine animal," the stablehand noted. "He 'as a powerful run."

"He has a fine lineage," Lucas replied.

"I will 'ave him saddled for you in a few minutes, Yer Grace." The stablehand took Dirk and walked him to the stable. A few minutes later, he returned with the grey, saddled. "He is spirited, Yer Grace."

"Thank you for the heads up. I will look forward to the ride," he said, hoisting himself up onto the saddle.

Lucas and his friends urged their horses, and the three of them rode away. Lucas found Colton spirited, but not overly, and managed him easily. As they approached fences, all three horses cleared them easily. There appeared to be no hesitancy, or lack of ability, as far as he could determine. Earlier that morning, he had sent an inquiry to a trainer in Newcastle, hoping to hear back soon.

The men slowed their horses to a canter as they headed back to the stable area.

"When do you plan to race him?" Romney asked.

"I would like to see him race in July if he appears ready. The colt has a fine gait and a strong run," Lucas returned.

"You will let me know. I plan to bet on him," added Clarendon. "The prospect of almost having a horse in the race excites me," he said with a laugh. "Charlotte would not approve of my owning one, but she would approve of you owning one."

"Why not?" Lucas asked and immediately regretted the question. Clarendon had been at his lowest point when he met his wife, Charlotte. His gambling and drinking had become excessive after his first wife died in childbirth.

"She feels it is best for me and for us," Clarendon said meaningfully.

"I spoke too soon, my friend. Forgive me," Lucas replied.

"Since finding Charlotte, my life feels new again. I will never forget Amelia, but I have learned how to remember the past and keep it in the past. I enjoy my present life and look forward to my future," Clarendon replied.

"My sister did that?" Romney asked, sounding a bit incredulous.

Clarendon raised an eyebrow in amusement. "She did. Your sister . . . *my wife* . . . is an amazing woman."

"Lady Clarendon would blush if she heard all of this," Lucas said, laughing. "I agree with you, Clarendon. You are in a good place." He reined the grey to a stop and waited for his friends to follow suit. "Who wants to ride Colton?"

"I would like to, if you are sure he will tolerate a different rider," Romney volunteered.

Clarendon said. "Perhaps I can take my turn tomorrow and give the boy a rest."

Lucas slid from the saddle, and Romney took his place and rode off. The two men waited for him. When he returned, Romney's excitement was palpable.

"How did it go?" they both asked.

"Colton is a wonderful horse. He reminds me so much of my horse—the one I rode until the battle. I hope I can find her one day," Romney said. "You have a winner there!"

As the three men approached the manor house, they noticed a coach pulling up to the front of the house. "It appears Lady Penfield's visit is to be a short one," Lucas grumbled to himself and spurred Colton toward the stables.

⫸⫷

"LADY PENFIELD, THANK you for agreeing to stop by," the duchess said, taking a seat on the yellow and white stripped chair.

"I should not stay too long, or I could rouse suspicions from Harriett, who is a most observant sister. She was still getting dressed when I left."

"Very well. I have been thinking about this, and feel we have a wonderful opportunity. As you know, Lucas recently became guardian to a distant cousin's two girls—you met them a few days ago. Cat . . . Lady Catherine . . . is a handful, I am afraid, and her shenanigans could be the unraveling of our plan. However, I confess to favoring her spunk," laughed the duchess. "A few days ago, she bound several of the chords of the pianoforte with ribbon—the very ribbon we had purchased in town! Her sister tried to play and a series of missed notes, muffled sounds came out of the instrument driving Mr. Whitesides, our new pianoforte master, to end that day's lesson."

The two women chuckled.

"She did not like the pianoforte, and this was her solution," tutted Lucas's mother.

"I like the girl, already!" Lady Penfield purred before picking up her teacup.

"Indeed! However, the man will probably request a higher price to his time," complained the duchess, although she would not mind paying it, as long as her plan came to fruition. Her son would never know the difference.

"Besides music, decorum and perhaps painting could fill their days. I realize the languages may have to wait for the governess. And if," she looked meaningfully at Lady Penfield, "all goes according to plan, the girls will have a more permanent guiding hand soon enough."

"My sister does a beautiful job of painting, including landscapes and people. I am lucky to get the landscape done correctly. However, I can stitch, and I would be happy to lend a hand there."

"That should be marvelous," clapped the duchess. This could work. "We will need to keep this between the two of us, alone."

"Of course! Harriett would have my head if she thought I was being manipulative, especially towards marriage. She has made a point of saying she does not plan to remarry."

"You mentioned that. It is not my business, of course, but can you share anything? I was always fond of your sister, as was my husband. If there had been something we could do . . . I know my husband tried, but even he was unsuccessful. Your father was most uncooperative, which I found highly uncharacteristic," said the duchess.

Lady Penfield looked away. "What he did was awful, but I cannot help but feel he has withheld something that would enable others to better understand, although I cannot determine what. His relationship with my sister suffered miserably. They barely speak more than what is necessary. I know I should not say that. It is a tribute to my sister that she insisted on coming home instead of going straight to the townhouse she received in London. It was unentailed and Lord Dudley had bequeathed it to her, as well."

"In Mayfair?" the duchess asked.

"Yes. I believe it is."

"Has she indicated when she plans to move to London?" the duchess queried, determination brewing.

"The only thing she has mentioned to me is her wish to find other property. She has not mentioned taking up the London residence yet. She wants to find something that has nothing to do with Lord Dudley," Lady Penfield explained.

"Good. I mean, good that she is not in a hurry," amended the duchess.

"Yes, it provides time. I would love to go shopping in London, however," Lady Penfield added.

"That would be an excellent outing. And of course, we can stay at our townhouse. You and your sister will be our guests! But first, we need to form a casual tutoring alliance. I shall let His Grace know that you and your sister have agreed to aide us with the girls—in these basic skills for a small period until we find a governess."

"If Harriett agrees. However, I think she already likes the girls. That will make it easier to gain her cooperation," conspired Lady Penfield.

"Be warned. Once my son knows your sister plans to assist the girls, he may react unfavorably and try to speed things up.

However, I shall endeavor to work through that," the duchess said, worried.

"I have the utmost confidence in you, Your Grace." Lady Penfield looked at the plate in front of her. "I cannot resist sticky buns, and I fear my resistance with these is waning. Would you mind if I discarded my gloves and ate one?"

"Help yourself, my dear!" she chuckled. "I must say, I have been trying my best not to take a second. But my resistance has disappeared. I worried that I might have both, so yes. *Please*, we are friends," the duchess said smoothly. She warmed the tea of her guest. "After you," she motioned toward the buns.

"Thank you," Lady Penfield said, unceremoniously popping a piece of the bun in her mouth. "They taste exactly like Chelsea buns!"

"These buns have always been my favorite." She stole a small piece of the remaining bun and delicately nibbled it. "I have a feeling there could be many more of these shared buns in our future!" the duchess said with a bright smile.

→≫≪←

As she returned to her room, Harriett asked Jane, who was making her bed, if she had seen her sister.

"Yes, my lady. I saw her leaving about twenty minutes ago. I heard her tell Watkins she was running a quick errand, as she left."

"How odd that she would leave saying nothing to me," murmured Harriett, picking up the sleeping Penelope from her bed pillow, which had become her favorite spot. The sisters had broken their fast together, and then Harriett had indicated the desire to read a book she had purchased a few days earlier, when they were in town.

"She seemed to be in a hurry," the maid added. "Likely she planned to be back before being missed."

"Perhaps," Harriett agreed, fighting back a troubling feeling. "Could you bring me some hot tea? The bruising and swelling on my ankle has subsided a great deal this past week, but it still aches. Perhaps some willow bark tea would help." She could not believe she had asked for the foul-tasting stuff, but she preferred it to the ankle pain.

"Yes, my lady." The maid started to leave but stopped. "Would Penelope enjoy a piece of toast? Cook always asks about her when I go to the kitchen," Jane asked.

"I think Penelope would like that. Our cook is such a caring woman. She always made sure my sister's pets and my own were well-fed, while growing up. I am not surprised she has latched onto Penelope. Knowing Alice, she probably introduced Cook to the puppy before me," she added with a chuckle.

"I will be happy to take care of that, my lady," Jane said, leaving the room and closing the door behind her.

The thought occurred to Harriett that the ache she was feeling may not have solely been her bruised ankle. She sat on her bed and closed her eyes. An unbidden image of Lucas came to mind . . . his liquid brown eyes looking down at her and warm arms holding her close—*very close*.

Abruptly shaking her head, her eyes shot open. What she was thinking about could never be again—not after what had happened between them. Perhaps she needed to leave Richmond and go to her townhouse in Mayfair, at least until her solicitor could secure a suitable country property for her. Forcing herself to relax, she leaned against the pillows lining her headboard and closed her eyes, determined to find a corner of her mind where he could not find her and where the pain in her heart did not exist.

CHAPTER ELEVEN

The next day

A TAP SOUNDED at the door, waking Harriett, and she rolled onto her back. Forcing open her eyes, she stared at the ceiling of her room. Rays of sunshine beaming through her window helped some. To herself, she admitted she felt a little better than she had last evening. The door opened and Jane walked in, carrying a cup of chocolate and some biscuits.

"Oh good! You're up, my lady. Yer sister asked if you could join her at the breakfast table. She said to let you know it was important."

"Alice is being a minx," she grumbled to herself, wondering why her sister felt able to walk into her room one day, but not the next. "If you can help me with my dress and hair, I will perform my ablutions and be down straight away." What in the world could be so important?

Harriett came down to the breakfast room and found her sister sitting reading the gossip sheet and laughing. She rested the walking stick next to the sidebar and began to fill her plate. "What's funny?" she asked, as she sat down across from Alice.

"Lady Peabody. You know . . . the one that always wears the enormous hat to church. I know it must be her because the description is spot on! Let me read this to you."

Excitement stirred Sunday morning's services (a week past) when a wild animal leaped from a mountain of fruit that sat upon a certain parishioner's head. The squirrel nearly made it through the entire service, but obviously decided to be the first to clear the heavy oaken doors into the sunshine. As the congregation finished the first verse of "Amazing Grace," the rodent leaped down from the cave of fruit, scattering its heady collection, and ran beneath a dozen pews before finally gaining its freedom into the sunshine. Surely, the squirrel was searching for the level of peace and salvation the song offers. This writer now peers into any loaded hat looking for wild animals since the incident.

Alice began laughing and almost choked on her food. "I am sorry. But every time I envision this, I wish I had been here," she said, wiping her mouth with her serviette.

"I was and I assure you, dear Lady Peabody did not know she had brought a guest. She did not even realize the gnawer escaped from *her* hat. I heard some men making assertions about how long the animal had been sleeping in the hat," she said with a giggle. "I wish you had been here. I would have laughed right along with you. As it was, I bit the inside of my cheek to keep from laughing. The woman sat directly in front of us. I saw him leap from her hat. It skimmed Mr. Nobbs's bald head and woke him up, just before he landed on Mrs. Nobbs's lap and ran under the pews. The whole thing was perfectly in time with the song."

Alice's eyes were wet with laughter. "I have missed being here with you, dear sister."

Harriett buttered her toast and added jam before looking up at her sibling. "What did you have to tell me? I feared it might be important and barely sipped my chocolate."

"Well . . ." she said, looking at Timmons who stood near the door.

"Timmons can be trusted," Harriett whispered. "Go on," she urged.

"I met with Her Grace yesterday," Alice began.

"Lucas's mother?" Harriett asked, dumbfounded. "Why would you do that?"

"She asked me to," Alice said simply, apparently ignoring her sister's slight pique as she spread jam on her own toast and popped a piece in her mouth before answering. "Mm! This apple jam is perfection!"

"The conversation," Harriett prompted.

"I have not forgotten. I merely wanted you to let me have my say first," Alice returned.

"Fine. Please, go on."

"As you know, they have two wards that the duke is now responsible to care for, and while they are searching for a governess, His Grace gave her leave to do whatever she could do to get the girls in lessons—whatever the expense."

"What has that to do with me?" Harriett demanded.

"Very little, but I assured the duchess that you would help. You will help, will you not?" Alice returned.

"What have you obligated me to do, Alice?"

"Help with their painting lessons. You do beautiful work, Harriett. And I plan to help with stitchery," Alice explained.

"What? You hate stitchery," scoffed Harriett, no longer concerned about whispering.

"I used to hate stitchery," hissed Alice. "I have a renewed interest in it. And you cannot deny that Mama has always deemed my stitchery flawless."

Harriett shook her head. Something was going on here, and it was more than met the eye. "If I go along with this plan, what are you thinking will be the result?" she pried.

"You are so suspicious. What plan? I cannot believe you would think so little of me," pouted her sister. "I have always had your best interest at heart. The duchess simply said she knew you painted well and needed someone that could help, and she noticed you got along famously with both girls," Alice asserted.

"What you say is true," admitted Harriett, carefully, still feeling suspicious. "They are both sweet young women, and I hate the hand they have been dealt. I think Luc . . . His Grace will do the responsible thing for both, but he cannot take the place of their mother. They will miss having both parents, naturally, but he cannot give them the same understanding or guidance their mother would have given," Harriett clarified.

"Will you agree to do it?" Alice prodded.

Harriett gave a long sigh. "I had not planned to stay that long, Harriett. How long is she asking for us to do this? I had hoped to be in my new home by spring—providing my solicitor finds one," she said, irritated.

"There is that . . . however, I believe the duchess intends a short-term obligation while they search for the right governess. I had not planned to stay long, either. We agree. Wait! Are you not planning to attend the Season in London?"

"I have not decided," Harriett returned, feeling pressed. If there had been an inkling that Lucas had any feelings, this would have been a simple decision. However, he made it clear he no longer cared for her. "I have just completed my mourning period."

"You can play the merry widow," teased her sister.

Harriett took her serviette and swatted her sister. "Silly! Do not let Mama hear you say something like that."

"You still have not answered," persisted Alice. "I think we could have great fun with the girls."

Harriett heaved a long sigh. "Fine. I will do it."

"You will not be sorry. These girls will love you, dear sister, and will flourish under your painting tutelage."

Harriett started at the rasher she had been moving around her plate and ate it, using that to punctuate this belabored conversation in her mind. "What are your plans today?"

"I promised the duchess I would notify her of your answer, but a penned note will be fine. I will write and send it quickly. Afterward, I thought we could go shopping," Alice answered, blithely.

Timmons cleared this throat, causing both sisters to look up.

"Your ladyships. Watkins asked that I deliver this note from Pembley Manor," he said, walking to Alice and holding out a silver salver.

"Interesting. It is as if the walls have ears!" muttered Harriett.

"Shush! You do not know what this could say, any more than I do," Alice purred, opening the note. "Is the courier still here?"

"Yes, your ladyship," Timmons replied.

"Ask him to wait for a reply," she bade. "She asks that we join her tomorrow, hoping that you have agreed to help."

Harriett regarded her sister and nodded. "I will do as you suggest. Let Her Grace know I look forward to it." She would meet the duchess and assess the situation for herself. Perhaps this was as Alice conveyed. "Since we will do that tomorrow, perhaps I should remain here today and continue to rest my ankle. It is improving, but I do not want to be on it longer than necessary and set the whole thing back. It has been rather irritating to be carried upstairs," she said in a low voice, glancing behind her to make sure Timmons was out of earshot.

"What if we sit in the greenhouse and read? Mama mentioned they had turned the greenhouse into more of an outdoor solarium since they had completed the orangery. She had instructed all the plantings to be moved out, except those used to decorate."

"I like that idea!" Harriett agreed. It was the first thing she had agreed with. Perhaps she would take Penelope with her and let the puppy enjoy herself. She had not spoken to Alice about the missive she had received from Dudley's heir and wished her opinion on that, as well.

"A MESSAGE FOR you, Your Grace," Egerton said, standing at the door of the duchess's parlor.

"Egerton, come in," the duchess said, placing a bookmark in

her book. She set the book where she had been sitting and stood. Reaching out, she took the letter on the small silver tray he extended to her. Her finger moved beneath the red waxed seal and opened the folded vellum.

"'Tis from Canton Manor. Our messenger received this and an answer to your earlier message. He said, it will delight Lady Dudley and Lady Penfield to join you tomorrow. He awaits in case there will be a reply or the need to send another message, Your Grace," Egerton added.

"Perfect! I shall inform Cook. Thank you, Egerton," the duchess said, reading the message. "She has accepted, good," she murmured.

"Pardon, Your Grace?" the butler queried.

"Nothing. I was only reacting to the note," she said distractedly. "Please send the footman back to his duties with my thanks."

The butler bowed and left the room.

"Wonderful! My plan seems to be working. Between them, it covers sewing and painting and a possible parent," she murmured contentedly to herself. She tucked the note into her pocket and picked up her book and sat down.

"Did you say something, Mother?" Lucas pushed the door open and walked into his mother's parlor.

His mother beamed. "I did, Son! I have taken you at your word and am planning for the girls to receive some of their lessons while we await your decision on a governess."

"Wonderful. Perhaps it will keep the two of them busy, especially the younger one. Beatrice seems able to occupy herself respectably. Cat is full of mischief," he said with a laugh. "She reminds me of . . ." he stopped and did not finish the sentence. He had been going to say Harriett.

His mother arched an eyebrow. "Yes . . . she shares the energy and passion of Lady Harriett," she ventured.

"Yes, so she does." He schooled his features. "The reason for my visit is the ladies. Lady Clarendon and Lady Romney are still here, and I had hoped you might arrange for a visit or whatever it is ladies do," he said.

"Son! Ladies *do* a lot," his mother gently corrected. "Did you have any other ideas for the group?" Her voice sounded faintly of sarcasm.

"I apologize, Mother. I did not mean to offend. I had noticed that the ladies have taken a trip into London one day and hoped to glimpse your plans for the rest of the week."

"They had asked that they have time to visit Madame Trousseau in London, so I have a few things planned since they have returned. They are delightful ladies and seem to understand it is not every day, you gain two young ladies to guide under your wing," she replied. "As it happens, I am organizing a breakfast for tomorrow with two other friends. They have already assured me both ladies plan to join us. They might enjoy my friends," she offered.

"Your invitation would be lovely, Mother. Neither Clarendon nor Romney have given an exact date—however, I think they still plan to stay another sennight. It is rare we see each other without the duties of Society. We are enjoying ourselves immensely."

"Delightful! Enjoy yourselves, son," she added.

"Thank you, Mother. What else do you have planned?" he wondered.

"The ladies seem to enjoy not having overly structured itineraries. They have been to London and have done much shopping around here. I only thought to keep their time feeling meaningful. If the weather holds, I thought croquet and a picnic would be fun."

He nodded and turned to leave.

"Son."

"Yes, Mother," he said, turning back.

"I was wondering if you would like to determine the abilities of the young women with horseback riding. That would allow me to gain a good understanding of what was still needed."

"I suppose that would be a good idea. They have both had

training. Perhaps I can bring them to the stables later tomorrow and see how they react to the horses. Have you commissioned riding habits for them?" he asked.

"I have. Cat grew bored, but Beatrice picked out fabric for one and I had the seamstress fashion one of the same style in a different color for Cat. I am not sure the girls share tastes in clothing, but we shall find out. I chose sedate greys and lavenders while they are in mourning," the duchess replied.

"Since we are in the country, I will relax some of the social mores around the mourning period for the girls, but I leave that up to you," he said, dipping his head.

"It is important that they understand the importance of them, so I am keeping them as close as possible to what is expected."

A small meow sounded from the stairwell, and both looked toward the door in time to see Cat and her kitten pass the parlor on their way to the kitchen.

"It is taking some time to get used to having an animal living in the house, although it seems a well-behaved kitten," the duchess murmured.

"It makes her happy. And she is doing a fine job—at least, she seems to be. I noticed her taking the kitten outside during the day, herself. It is gaining her friends among the staff, for certain, since they are aware the responsibility would fall to them otherwise."

"I do not think they mind. They seem to adore the girls. It is nice to have young people in the manor house again," she said, smiling wistfully up at her son. "I try not to get carried away in remembrances, but it is not too difficult to recall you at Cat's age—you with your friends Matthew, Christopher and Evan."

He laughed. "Life was a grand adventure for us, then. The swimming in the pond, horseback races, and fishing . . . You gave me an idea, Mother. Thank you!"

"You are welcome," she answered, opening her book up and moving the place holder.

He gave a quick bow and left the room. He and his friends

had not gone fishing in an age. The weather was crisp, but not overly cold—which would matter little, anyhow.

Walking upstairs to his game room, he heard laughter over the smack of the billiard balls coming from the room. Opening the door, he leaned against the doorjamb. "How do you feel about packing a hearty lunch and going fishing?"

"Splendid idea! I have not been fishing in an age," Clarendon said.

"Me either," Romney chimed in. "Well, the last time was in New Orleans with Bethany, but that was completely different."

"Your *wife* fishes?" Clarendon asked. "I guess she would. I had not considered that. She is extremely accomplished."

"When I met her, her grandmother had gone to visit her aunt. I had just come off the battlefield with my injuries and could offer no help. She provided sustenance for both of us, on her own."

Clarendon shook his head. "Your story still amazes us all, and we are happy you met Bethany. You've done well for yourself."

Both men regarded Lucas.

"Please do not feel sorry for me. I am happy as I am," he rejoined.

"You have nothing to worry about where Clarendon and I are concerned. We are not matchmakers, I assure you," Romney hooted. "What are the stakes for fishing?"

"You want to wager?" Lucas said.

"I do! The winner gets to ride Colton later. The person that pulls in the biggest fish—not the most. We will release them, of course," Clarendon suggested.

"Shall we make it a couples' competition?" Romney suggested. "Now that you know my wife's abilities."

"No! Your wife could put us all to shame. I had hoped to ride that horse," Clarendon remarked, laughing.

"You really like my horse!" Lucas said, nodding. "I agree with the wager. My only stipulation is, if someone has already ridden too much for him, we wait for tomorrow."

"Sounds perfect," Lucas said. "Meet me downstairs in ten. I'll make the arrangements."

Fifteen minutes later, the three men were on their horses and headed in the direction of the stream that ran through the back of the property. It did not take long on horseback to reach their favorite childhood spot. Tall, hardwood trees shaded the area, and the big rock they always left their clothes beneath taunted them.

"No! Do not go there," Lucas said when he spied Romney looking at the rock with a sly smile.

"I promise . . . I am not thinking about swimming. It is too cold," his friend said, laughing. "Besides, I would have a terrible time explaining that to Bethany, whose image of Englishmen is much more rigid. I think our group has already challenged her."

They all guffawed.

"I brought plenty of food for us," Lucas offered, as he slid from the horse. "Recognize these?" He held out the fishing poles.

"Are those the same poles we used as boys?" Romney asked.

"They are. I kept them. My father fashioned them for us, and it was that part of my father—where he could take the time with my friends and me, that I miss the most," Lucas lamented.

As they approached the high rock near the stream, Lucas slid down and secured his horse. The other men followed suit, each man taking a pole with his initials etched in them—something they had done on one of the many holidays from Eton they had taken together.

Relaxation was exactly what Lucas needed, considering the direction his life had taken this past week. Things always felt easier with his friends. The three of them baited their fishing poles and took the spot they felt gave the best advantage for catching the biggest fish . . . and waited.

Romney broke the quiet first. "I seem to recall a time when you and I had to scramble for a tree branch," he began.

Clarendon chimed in. "I've heard this story and never tire of it. A certain young woman and her sister stole your clothing.

What I would love to know is: did they hang around to see you look for them?"

"I never thought the giggling in the tree line was a covey of doves!" laughed Romney.

"How close is Lord Scarsdale's property to yours?" Clarendon asked.

How had he forgotten the incident? "His property adjoins on the other side of the steam." He pointed down the stream and they could see a small walking bridge extending over the water. *Harriett had been out of his life for years . . . and suddenly, she was everywhere.* Lucas needed to see her, if for nothing else, to rid her from his life once and for all.

CHAPTER TWELVE

"**R**EMEMBER WHEN WE used to explore as children?" Harriett leaned back on the chaise her mother had installed in the greenhouse—which looked more like a glass room from a fairytale. Her mother had installed plants along the walls, a worn Aubusson carpet on the floor, and she had hung a discarded crystal chandelier from the ceiling. Harriett recognized it as the one that used to be in the dining room as a child.

"I remember that you always got us into trouble—usually doing something we were not supposed to do," quipped Alice.

"Not always!" Harriett swatted her sister playfully with the rolled-up gossip rag they had brought with them. "I can remember there was one time you got us in a lot of trouble!"

"Shhh! As you say, these walls may have ears," retorted Alice.

"Oh, my goodness! Your husband would love to learn of the antics you did as a young girl," bantered Harriett. "You were forever dragging me into one thing or another—and Father would become upset with me."

"Yes . . . but we did not tell him of *all* our adventures," Alice reminded her. "Recall the high rock by the stream? If I recall correctly, that mischief was your idea. We barely made it back over the bridge before being caught."

Harriett furrowed her brow, silently spinning through memories, hoping to recall what her sister was speaking of. The image of the tall rock with discarded male clothing stacked in two small stacks came to mind. The boys that had been wearing them were splashing around in the water ahead of them, oblivious to their presence. She had persuaded her sister to follow her and the two of them had crawled around on all fours and pulled the clothing to the back of the rock, barely able to contain their mirth. "We hid in the tree and watched!" snorted Harriett, evoking what she had seen at twelve. "You are right! I had not thought about that day in an age!"

Alice guffawed. "Yes . . . and I never saw one of those *again* until my marriage night."

Harriett's eyes widened at her sister's candor and burst into giggles, her eyes running with tears. "Alice, we were so brazen as young girls. That would have surely merited a paddling if they had caught us."

"I have often wondered how we got away with it!" Alice declared. "Have you been the high rock since?"

A furious blush crept up Harriett's neck.

"Dear goodness. *You have!*" Alice chided, folding her arms across her chest. "Tell me!"

"I should not say . . ." Harriett began, "but once, Lucas took me there."

"The two of you went there . . . *alone?*"

Harriett nodded. She remembered that afternoon very well.

"You were always such a goody-good! Had Father known you were alone with Lucas, he would have made you marry . . ." Alice stopped short. "I apologize for saying that, Harriett."

Harriett fell quiet for a minute. "The irony was, we did nothing, and he was planning to marry me. They were some of the happiest moments of my life until my life changed."

"Whatever in the world motivated Father to do such a thing? He and Mother used to be so close, so loving. But when he sent you away, things changed in the house," Alice said sadly. "Father spent many more hours in his office, and they argued."

"I had not realized things had changed at home until I arrived.

Mama and Father are so distant with each other. I suspected it had to do with my marriage." She looked at her sister and saw her swipe a tear from her cheek. "It must have been difficult here."

"I do not know why Father did that to you, but his life changed, too... all of our lives did," Alice replied.

Impulsively, Harriett sat up on her chaise and stepped over to her sister, giving her a hug. "I missed everyone so. Dudley was an awful husband, but he is gone, now, and I am here. I hope that we can spend lots of time together, Al. I missed you, most of all."

"I missed you, too, Harriett," Alice said, grinning through tears and swiping at her face. "I hope you will find a house close by, although I have not wanted to press you for anything. My purpose in coming was to spend time with the sister I have dearly missed."

Harriett looked down and studied her hands. "I need your advice, Al."

Her sister angled her head and took her sister's hands in hers. "Anything."

"I received a missive the other day . . . from Dudley's heir. He says he needs to see me." She shuddered involuntarily.

"You cannot go back there!" she cried. "I will not allow it. Father . . ."

"Would not have anything to say," Harriett said, cutting in. "Father got me into this for reasons I have never fathomed. I want nothing to do with Dudley's family."

"Could this have something to do with his death?" Alice asked.

Harriett pulled her hands out of her sister's and went silent. She could not relive that night, yet, she had never told a soul about it. Her sister could be trusted, she reasoned. But if she let one person know, her secret might no longer haunt her. "If I tell you something, can you swear to never tell a person?"

"I promise, Harriett," Alice said, swinging her feet to the floor. "But I cannot help you if you do not tell me."

"I *want* to tell you . . . I swear I do. It's just that I have had no one to trust in so long."

Alice pulled her sister into an embrace. "It's all right if you don't want to talk about it now."

"Alice, he died instantly when his horse threw him."

"I know," her sister said.

"Maybe what you do not know is that we had argued." Harriett turned away.

"His death was not your fault, Harriett."

"I am not sure others would think the same thing," Harriett murmured. "I was the reason he left to ride his horse."

"I am not following this," Alice began, but stopped. She lifted her sister's chin. "Did he hurt you?"

Harriett wanted to tell Alice. And if she did not do it now, she would lose all courage. "He would hurt me intentionally when he . . ."

Her sister's face paled. "What do you mean?"

"I mean, he always hurt me, when he . . ." Guilt-tinged memories of that last night flooded her mind. "I was reading in my room, and he pushed open the door and slammed it behind him. He had been drinking. I bade him to leave me alone, to find someone else. He had a mistress, and for a while he would leave me alone. But not that night."

Alice sat quietly, waiting.

"He threw me to the bed, but I cried and begged him to leave me alone. He grew angry and left, swearing at me. He had been drinking. The magistrate came to the door hours later and told me they had found his body."

"How does that implicate you in his death, Sister?"

"If it had not been for my rejection, he would still be here," Harriett said.

"Yes, but that is supposition. You rejected his abuse. You did nothing wrong," Alice reminded her, rubbing Harriett's back.

"I was never more surprised to find out he had left me provided for in the event of his death. I believe he loved me in the only way he could love—by possession. I moved to the dowager house and stayed there for exactly one year. I left by the cover of night. And now, they are looking for me."

"Who are *they*? And what do you mean *they* are looking for you?" Alice asked.

Harriett reached into her pocket and pulled out the note, handing it to her sister.

After reading it, Alice looked up. "What could Dudley's heir possibly want with you?"

◆》》》《《《◆

HE SHOULD HAVE known better than to bet against Romney. All the time spent in America and in between apparently taught him the finer art of fishing. He reeled them in as if he were whispering to them, *"Take my hook, I'll let you go."* Lucas laughed to himself as he made his way downstairs.

"Your Grace, will you be back for dinner?" the tall, grey butler asked, holding out his greatcoat.

"Thank you, Egerton. I have a brief meeting in Richmond and should be back in a few hours." Lucas took his hat, put it on his head and scurried down the steps, pleased to see his coach waiting. He and his friends had returned a little over an hour ago to a hot luncheon. Both Romney and Clarendon were spending some time with their wives, while he attended a meeting with his solicitor.

Once the girls had settled in, he realized he still needed to review the documents of the guardianship, and assumed from what he saw, that little funds had been available to provide for the girls. It mattered not. He had plenty of blunt and intended to make provisions in his will for them. Once this was done, he would breathe easier. They needed to know they were wanted.

His coach slowed in front of a small three-storied brown building on High Street and Lucas made his way upstairs to the first floor. The building was stark, with minimal furnishings. It was the exact opposite of Mr. Innes's office, which was a lavish copy of his London office.

The lawyer had several clients in the area and had seen fit to establish a small office in Richmond, and routinely came in every two weeks for a day or two. It served Lucas's purposes, as he would rather meet the man here on one of his visits than travel to London for spur-of-the-moment things. As much as he loved his mother, with his lawyer not visiting the house, she knew nothing was afoot, and he avoided her questions. His mother was not the type to skirt an issue if she desired to know something.

He opened the door and was greeted by a lanky, bespeckled young man. "Welcome, Your Grace. Mr. Innes is expecting you in his office."

"You must be Innes's new law clerk he mentioned," Lucas said. "I hope you are enjoying the work."

"Very much so, Your Grace," the man replied as he escorted Lucas to Innes's office. Lucas walked into a lavishly appointed room with rich leather and walnut chairs. Mr. Innes's desk nearly dwarfed the shorter man with its size, which always amused Lucas. From his own height of six feet, he wondered if the desk compensated for the lawyer's lack of physical stature. Innes could not be over five-and-a-half feet tall, with a rotund belly and a balding pate. What Innes lacked in physical stature, he more than made up for with his professional reputation.

"Good afternoon, Your Grace." The man stepped from around his desk and opened a carved liquor cabinet in the corner. "Can I offer you anything to drink?"

"I would like that, Innes. Brandy, if you have it," Lucas said.

Reaching in, the solicitor extracted two glasses and a decanter. He gave a decent measure to Lucas and gave himself only a small amount.

"Thank you," Lucas said, sipping the amber liquid. "I trust you deciphered the ideas in my letter."

"I did," Innes said. "My condolences on the loss of your cousin and his wife. Influenza is a nasty business."

"The girls have settled into the estate. As near as I can tell, aside from a spinster aunt—a sister to my cousin—there were few options for care of the girls," Lucas explained.

The solicitor passed two documents his way. "This is the crux of the guardianship. Most of your cousin's money went to keep up his household, which will remain with his sister, until she passes—at which time, it will go to his eldest daughter, Lady Beatrice."

"I see. Please add ten thousand pounds for each of the girls into their dowry," Lucas said. "They are my wards, and they will be treated as members of the family."

The older man removed his spectacles and placed them on his desk and regarded Lucas. "That is extremely generous, Your Grace." He fumbled through some papers until he found what he needed and held it up. "Their father left them a thousand pounds each but based on what I understand from his estate paperwork, I believe it was more than he could spare."

Lucas mulled this over. But for the accident of birth, he too, could have easily been the man without funds. "Eleven thousand pounds for a dowry seems the wrong number. Round them both up to fifteen thousand pounds. They are my family, now, and I will do for them that which I had intimated in my verbal agreement with their father. I will care for them. Should anyone ask—although I cannot see how it would be their business—five thousand of it came from their parents," he stated. "If there are additional monies for their maintenance, divide it into individual accounts with their names on it. I would like to have access to both accounts to add a small monthly amount, and a monthly accounting of the account values, along with the rest of my estate. Do you think fifty pounds a month for each girl, increased to a hundred on their sixteenth birthday, sufficient until they marry? Upon that date, all monies remain in their name."

"That is most generous, Your Grace," the man slid the spectacles onto his nose and, with a wiggle of his nose, nudged them in place. "I assume you do not plan to discuss this with the girls."

"No."

"Good. It will give the money time to accumulate, if they do not have immediate access to it."

"Miss Beatrice is my first concern, as her coming out will be this Season, following her mourning period. My mother has discussed shortening it to six months to give the girl a chance to become comfortable in Society," Lucas replied, a thoughtful expression drawing his brows together. "I have one more small clarification, and I look to your expertise here. To title them as *lady*, they would have to be my natural or adopted daughters, correct?" Lucas had pondered adoption, if things continued to work out, but realized the girls could see that as erasing their parents, so he had nixed that.

"You are correct, Your Grace. I can see that could be a di-lemma, and there may be those that use the wrong title," Innes responded.

"I wanted to clarify, in case the subject arises." Lucas hoped it would not. He suspected they would be happy with their new circumstances and would not want for anything. "Please also make the adjustments to my will, detailed in my letter, in the event of my untimely demise."

"I have done that, Your Grace, and will update the directives we discussed today in the document," Innes said. "Your kindness and understanding with these children . . . these young wom-en . . . go beyond what most would consider," the lawyer continued. "I will see these provisions inserted and will messen-ger the documents to your attention at their completion. Shall we meet again in a fortnight for signatures?"

"That is a fine plan," Lucas said, rising to his feet. "If that is all, I can take my leave."

The man stood and gave a quick bow of his head. "Thank you, Your Grace."

Lucas left the building feeling good about what he had ac-complished. He had secured the future of his wards. Crossing the street, a strong breeze hit, and he noticed the woman leaving the mercantile trying to hold on to her hat. Her footman had stepped away to deposit a taller pile of packages into a carriage parked nearby. He squinted against the afternoon sun and recognized the woman. *Lady Harriett Dudley.* Earlier, with his friends, he had wished to see her. The mystical force of the wind gave an unnerving sense his imagination had conjured her presence.

Propelled by his feet and absent good sense, he hurried across the street to her side. "Lady Dudley, can I be of assistance?"

Her eyebrows shot up in surprise at his appearance. "I would never have expected to see you here, Your Grace," she answered in a surprised tone.

Determined not to allow what must have been surprise to mar the moment, he attempted to be jovial. "I saw the wind nearly carry you off a moment ago, and my chivalrous nature took charge."

She raised her eyes to his face. "You startled me almost as much as the wind, which came out of nowhere!"

"I had the same thought," he agreed with a teasing smile.

"If you truly do not mind, I had hoped to make a couple of purchases in the bookstore. I would welcome your assistance," she replied. "I am looking for instructional books on painting."

Curiosity piqued his interest, but Lucas ignored the impulse to ask for clarification. There could be any number of reasons she was looking for such a thing. What he found harder to ignore was *her.* He had not considered the possibility of running into her while meeting his solicitor. Clearing his throat, he asked, "Would you like to stop at the confectionary for a Chelsea bun?" In that moment, it was all he could think of, and hoped the shop had them.

The doorbell to the mercantile shop rang and her sister came out. "Your Grace," she cooed, looking from one to the other. She glanced at her sister. "I found the thread I needed. The shop owner had an extra spool of it in the back." She dangled the small package in front of them.

"His Grace has asked us to join him for a bun," Harriett said, evading his eyes.

Alice smiled. "I am sure he meant you, and not both of us, Harriett. Besides, I need to ask a question of Mrs. Thimblesby. I shall join you in the bookstore," she said, indicating the store three doors down with a tilt of her head. "Your Grace." Alice gave a polite incline of her head and retreated to the modiste's shop at the opposite end of the street, leaving Harriett standing there with him in front of the confectionary.

Lucas had the distinct impression he had just been outmaneuvered, but to what end? Her sister stopped at the carriage and spoke with the driver, nodding briefly in his direction, before continuing to the modiste's.

A look of confusion passed over Harriett's face.

"Shall we?" he asked, extending his arm.

She nodded and politely placed her gloved hand on his arm, sending a wave of awareness through him.

He led her to a small table in the sweet shop and waved one server over their way. "We would like Chelsea buns, if you have them, and two cups of chocolate."

"Aye, we do, Yer Grace," beamed the server, who gave a quick curtsy and scurried off to do his bidding.

"You remembered," Harriett said, watching him.

"I remember everything. That may be my problem." He searched her gaze, briefly losing himself in her green eyes. "So much went unanswered, Harriett. I felt like I was past the anger and the . . ." He stopped himself before he said more. "Would you consider going riding with me, like we used to?" Fresh air and the freedom to say what they should have been able to say years ago—what he needed to say—without servants overhearing, or worse . . . his mother, was what they needed.

She studied him for a minute before finally answering. "I will. I have plans for tomorrow. Perhaps the day after?"

"I would like that." He wanted to say more, but the server appeared with their order. She placed a cup of chocolate in front of each of them, and a single Chelsea bun between them. "Yer

Grace, I apologize for bringing ye only one, but we have had a run on these buns today. Two men and their wives came in earlier and bought them all save this one. Would ye be able to share it?"

Lucas looked to Harriett, before answering, relieved she smiled and nodded her ascent. But now he was curious. "May I ask what the man that purchased them looked like?"

"Handsome they were—one with dark brown hair and blue eyes and the other blond. They both had their wives with them, which kept me on me best behavior," the young woman teased with eyes full of mirth. "Ye just missed them," she added, pointing behind him, in the direction of his home.

Lucas wondered what Harriett thought about the young woman's candor, but noticed she was still smiling at him.

"What time shall I expect you?" she asked.

CHAPTER THIRTEEN

The next day
Pembley Manor

W HAT IN THE world had possessed him to ask Harriett to ride horses with him? Lucas had not felt like such a ball of nerves since he had been in school. Five years ago, she had disappeared without a word. Her father had traded her for some sort of debt, although no details had ever been forthcoming. Now she was back—a widow, no less—and her presence tortured him. So, what did he do? Invited her out for sweet treats, followed by a ride across his vast estate on horseback.

His two friends and their wives entered the room. Lucas was certain they had gone to Town yesterday, together, although it was curious that no one mentioned the trip while they were together during the afternoon. Perhaps it was a spur-of-the-moment decision. He waved the footman over. "Ladies, would you enjoy a pitcher of chocolate?"

Lady Romney glanced at Lady Clarendon, who nodded. "Yes," she smiled. "I am not used to this, but can quickly grow accustomed."

Romney inclined his head, and the footman left to bring the drink.

He turned to his friend. "How were the Chelsea buns, Romney?"

His friend shot him a puzzled look. "How did you know?" Romney drawled. "Do you have spies in the town?"

"No. I stopped at the confectionary after my appointment with my solicitor and they described you perfectly. The young server told me you bought every Chelsea bun in the place," he said, chuckling.

Clarendon filled his plate and found a seat. "Romney swears he will take his time eating them. There must be two dozen!"

"My lovely wife mentioned she might like to try them," Romney offered, as he buttered his toast. "So, I purchased a few. And did I mention they have also become my favorite treat?"

"How did you know?" Clarendon said, winking at their friend, Romney.

"What do you mean, how did I know?" He took a bite of his brioche and noticed the table had gone quiet.

"We saw her," Clarendon finally said. "Of course, Charlotte and Lady Romney did not know her, but Romney and I recognized Lady Dudley. And we saw your coach . . . and figured . . ."

"Nothing happened," Lucas insisted, taking a sip of his coffee.

"So, you saw Lady Dudley?" Romney asked.

Lucas laid down his utensils and looked at his friends. "Yes. She has agreed to go riding with me this afternoon. I did it to provide closure. We could never speak about what happened. I thought it would help us resolve the past. Nothing more. What we might have had once can never be."

"I understand, Lucas," Clarendon said.

"I do as well, my friend. I hope it helps. Sorry to have teased you," Romney added.

From the corner of his eye, Lucas noticed the ladies give each other a questioning look.

"Where do you intend to take her?" Romney inquired.

"I thought I would take the grey and one mare and ride around the property. There is no specific place in mind," Lucas said. "Do me a favor. Do not mention this to my mother. It would give her hope where there is none."

"You have my word," Romney said.

"Mine, too," Clarendon added. "Good luck."

"Lady Romney and I plan to join your mother for a meal today," Lady Clarendon said.

"Mother is looking forward to it."

"As are we," Lady Clarendon added.

The sound of swishing skirts preceded his mother's entrance. "Hello, everyone. I am late this morning." She glanced at her son and a smile creased her face. After ladling some fruit on her plate, the duchess sat down next to the two young countesses. A footman came and filled her teacup. "You are all quiet. What did I miss?"

⇒⇒⇒⇒≪≪≪≪

HARRIETT AWOKE EARLY and lay in her warm bed, staring at the lace canopy over her bed. Conflicted, she dreaded putting her foot onto the cold floor beneath her, but looked forward to the day, especially the afternoon. If she had her druthers, she would skip to that part.

Jane entered and began the morning's dressing routine. She helped her into her navy dress of silk and wool. Folds of ecru-colored silk net trimming lined the neck and sleeves. Jane pulled her hair back into a low chignon, with small curls around her face. Harriett opted for a light serving of chocolate and toast, trying to quell the butterflies that had taken root in her stomach.

Harriett had made no mention of today's meeting when she saw Lucas yesterday, unsure of how he might react. Admittedly, she liked Miss Cat and Miss Beatrice; however, she felt pressured by her sister. She did not know the time required and feared by agreeing to help, she might have obligated herself to staying here much longer than originally planned.

"Are you ready?" Alice asked, gliding into Harriett's room

and sitting in one of the mahogany armchairs in front of the fireplace. She picked up the small pillow and sat it in her lap, fingering the worn fringe. "Today will be the first day you leave your cane behind."

"Yes. I have been debating whether to give it a 'go' without the cane. I shall be on my feet quite a bit," Harriett mused.

"When you are finished with it, you can prop it against the fireplace, like Grandmama used to do when she was around," Alice suggested with a sly look.

Harriett quirked a brow and grinned. "It will seem as if she was here with me. If I smell her sweet perfume, I shall know she is!"

"Grandmama was a sweet woman. I still miss her," reflected her sister. "She would be happy you have taken her room." Harriett dismissed Jane and came to sit in the other chair.

"You have an unusual look on your face, dear sister," Alice observed.

"Yes. Well, I might as well tell you. You will know it soon enough, anyway," Harriett began. "Lucas asked me to go riding with him this afternoon."

Alice gripped her sister's hands. "This is wonderful news! I had a feeling about yesterday."

"Do not put too much into this, Alice. He only wants to ask me some questions—most likely about my disappearance. He mentioned that he had reconciled me to his past, and until my appearance, everything seemed fine. But since saving me a week ago, he needs more answers."

Alice clapped gleefully. "Go on . . ."

"There really is nothing more to say, although I confess, I look forward to the ride." Her gaze locked with her sister's. "I also wonder what you have gotten me into with his young wards. You know my plans are to move on to London very soon, or to my new home, should my solicitor find what I require."

"I wish you . . ." Alice began.

"Perhaps we should depart," Harriett said, grabbing her reticule and her hat.

An hour later, Harriett fought back the butterflies in her stomach. As the wheels crunched over the familiar pebbled drive, she drew in a breath, unsure she could hide her nervousness. She had not been to Lucas's home in over five years.

"Lady Penfield, Lady Dudley. Welcome. Her Grace is expecting you in her parlor," the aging butler said, taking Harriett and Alice's wraps. "Please follow me."

The door to the parlor opened, and the duchess stood and walked to the door to welcome her guests. "Ladies, thank you so much for coming."

Harriett spotted the two ladies sitting on the parlor couch. She could not recall meeting them before. A beautifully appointed table had been placed in the center of the room.

"I must present to you these lovely ladies—Lady Romney and Lady Clarendon," the duchess said. Each lady inclined their head as they were introduced. "Ladies, we have the sisters Scarsdale, Lady Penfield, and Lady Dudley."

"It is our pleasure to meet you both," Lady Clarendon said, in turn.

"Ladies, perhaps we should take our seats," the duchess said, indicating the table in the center of the room.

"What a lovely setting, Your Grace," Harriett offered.

"Thank you," the duchess said, inclining her head as she waited for Lady Dudley to be seated. As she placed the serviette on her lap, she continued, "As you know, my son has become guardian to two lovely young ladies. A distant cousin and his wife succumbed to influenza. While we search for a governess, I had hoped to garner help in keeping the girls occupied."

Speaking to Harriett and Alice, the duchess explained her goal. "You have already met them both in town the other day. Lady Beatrice is sixteen and we plan to present her to Society following her mourning. Lady Catherine is twelve. Both young women are delightful."

"My sister mentioned your interest in securing time painting with the girls," Harriett ventured, finally feeling the butterflies ease from her stomach.

"Yes, my dear. And as I recall, you have a wonderful eye and see the intricacies in nature," the duchess rejoined. "I believe the girls would enjoy your instruction. Miss Catherine has an interest in nature, particularly animals. She might appreciate learning to paint them. We could not assess much of what they know, yet."

"I would be most happy to do that. I found both young ladies a delight when I met them at the modiste's," Harriett replied, pleased that she might not have to paint scenery. She preferred to paint horses and other animals.

"I would be happy to help with stitchery," Alice volunteered.

Harriett noted that there seemed to be a friendship between the duchess and her sister, although she had never heard Alice mention anything. However, she had been gone for five years and life went on here without her.

"That would be lovely, Lady Penfield," the duchess replied. She looked at Ladies Romney and Clarendon. "I realize you ladies are planning to leave soon, however, if you have talents you wish to share that can help with the girls, I would be most appreciative. Hopefully, my son will be successful in securing a governess soon."

Lady Clarendon looked at Lady Romney before speaking. "We could be persuaded to stay a day or two more, although I am not sure I have any special talents to laud. Perhaps I can assist Lady Penfield with stitchery. Lady Romney, however, has a great knowledge of plants and herbs that could be beneficial—I know her knowledge probably saved her husband's life when they were in America."

Lady Romney looked at Lady Clarendon as she spoke. "I would be happy to help for a short time."

A small tap sounded at the door to the parlor and Miss Catherine opened it and stepped into the room. "Your Grace, I apologize for the intrusion, but I believe Greyson is hiding in here. He was following me upstairs and disappeared on this floor.

I have searched everywhere."

"Your kitten?" the duchess asked, her voice a tad higher than it had been a few moments earlier.

"Yes, ma'am. I am terribly sorry for the intrusion." Before anyone could say anything, the girl got to her knees and began crawling around the room, calling the kitten, and looking under the tables and chairs.

"Miss Catherine," retorted the duchess in a calm voice. "Perhaps the kitten made its way upstairs." She turned to the group of women. "You remember Miss Catherine? Darling girls—and as I alluded to, very interested in animals."

Frustration bloomed on the duchess's face and Harriett decided to assist, lest the girl be tendered to the nearest orphanage. "Allow me to help, Your Grace. I miss having kittens around." Without waiting for an answer, she stood and began searching. The rest of the women followed suit, and soon, they were everywhere, searching beneath the folds of the curtains, looking in a small corner of book stacks, and peering under the furniture in the large room.

Harriett glanced up when she heard a faint meow coming from the direction of the door and scurried toward it. That was when she noticed the duke standing in the door, watching. Unable to hold back, she laughed out loud as she realized the scene before him, imagining what he must have thought. Her bark of laughter brought all the heads in the room upright and focused on the two of them. At the same time, she spotted a small fluff of grey hair behind the door and scooped it up.

"I believe this is yours, Miss Catherine," she said, handing the mewing kitten to the young girl. She glanced at Lucas and saw an amused smile playing at his lips.

"What a curious sight to behold," he said, grinning and nodding at the room. "Until Lady Dudley picked up the kitten, I imagined this to be some new ladies' game."

Everyone stood and remained where they were.

Harriett noticed the duke glance toward his mother, whose

face was one of pure annoyance. He must have attributed her displeasure to his remarks, because his own expression immediately changed from mirth to vexation. He cleared his throat. "Miss Catherine, please bring the kitten with you to my study. Mother, I apologize for the intrusion."

As he moved to close the door, his gaze locked on Harriett's, sending a delicious feeling of warmth down her spine. "It is an unexpected pleasure to see you and your sister here," he added before finally inclining his head and closing the door.

Harriett noticed a subtle, wordless exchange between her sister and the duchess before Her Grace finally spoke. She made a mental note to discuss this with Alice later.

"Ladies, I apologize for this unfortunate mishap. Now you see why I welcome your help. These lovely girls must have productive things to occupy their time until we can secure a governess. Miss Catherine has many energetic interests, which I am hoping to channel into skills that will carry her forth in Society," she said with a practiced smile. "Thank you for agreeing to help! I appreciate each of you."

"I certainly do not mind," Harriett said. "I think I will enjoy spending time with Miss Catherine. She reminds me a bit of myself at that age. In fact, I picked up some painting supplies in town, after Alice informed me of your request for help, Your Grace."

"Excellent!" The duchess clapped her hands. "I am more hopeful than ever that things will work out beautifully!"

Harriett noticed another quick glace between the other three ladies and the duchess. She sensed she had missed something in the duchess's remarks but was unsure what it could have been.

Chapter Fourteen

Later that day

Lucas arrived at Canton Manor several hours later in a carriage. He had spent an hour or more trying to decide whether to ride Dirk there and have Harriett's horse saddled—which could create even more questions than just picking her up. He looked forward to it, especially after seeing her in the beautiful navy confection she wore to visit his mother.

He planned to speak to his mother later—he was a little unnerved by Harriett's appearance there. He had to admit, the episode had been funny. He had not known Lady Harriett Dudley was one of the women his mother was tapping to help with the girls. Clearly, Cat needed guidance, and he would not stop his mother. However, what Lucas intended to do was hire the first reasonable governess that he met!

Cat had apologized repeatedly for her lapse of judgement. However, something about the young lady's sincerity rang false, although he was still wont to figure it out. One question she had asked gave him pause. She had asked about Lady Dudley and how he knew her, and then went to lengths to say how much she liked her. He shrugged to himself. Perhaps he was making too much of it, based on his own sensitivities, where Harriett was concerned.

As his coach pulled up, a footman met him.

"I am here to see Lady Dudley," he said.

"Very good, Your Grace. She asked that we send you to her mother's parlor."

Making his way up the steps, a dour-faced butler greeted him and bade him follow to the parlor. He was not sure who would be in there to greet him, so he steeled himself as the door opened and his arrival was announced.

"Good afternoon, Your Grace," Harriett said.

She was beautiful, dressed in a rich burgundy riding habit with a stylish feathered hat. "I did not ask if we would ride our own horses, so I put the stable on alert, just in case."

"I just purchased a young steed that I would like to prepare for the track—eventually. I thought I could ride him today."

"Not Dirk? What a slight for that poor horse," she teased.

"Not really. I have ridden him all over the continent. He takes any opportunity to rest. I prefer him to any horse, of course. However, I thought to show my grey off to you if you will indulge me."

Harriett smiled up at him and, in that moment, Lucas thought he caught an expression of longing. But that would be too much to hope. Besides, he was no longer interested, he told himself. His heart had mended, and he had moved on.

"Then, let us see your grey. You had mentioned your interest in owning a racehorse years ago. I would like to see the young horse that could take you to that finish line," she returned.

He walked her to the carriage and helped her inside. Once she was seated, he entered and sat facing her.

"Where will we ride?" she asked in a low voice.

He realized how awkward this ride must be for her after all these years. Hell's teeth, it was for him. But he had so much to ask, and since seeing her almost a fortnight ago, he had done nothing but think of her. It had to end. "You always enjoyed the area around the stream that intersects our property. I thought we might ride in that direction. The land is less rocky and there are large sections of flat land on which we can run the horses," he answered. He stared into her eyes until she averted her gaze.

"I remember it well," she murmured, looking out the window.

My God, what am I doing? She will run from me in a matter of minutes if I keep this up.

"I noticed you are without a cane and did not limp. I take it your ankle has healed?" he asked, deciding this was a safe topic.

"It has, Your . . . Lucas," she replied.

"I appreciate that you have called me Lucas. I do not wish things to be so awkward between us," he began. They had arrived at his estate. He said nothing more, hoping they had said enough to break the tension.

As his carriage stopped at his stables, he started to the door, intending to assist her from the carriage, but was surprised to see Frank, his head groom, open it. The man always favored Lady Dudley to his other guests. He wondered how the man knew she was in the carriage, until he spotted a low, square basket and blanket near the horses, which were waiting for them.

"'Tis good to see ye again, milady," the older man said, placing a step for her to alight from the carriage.

"Frank! How do you do? It is so good to see you again. I hope your wife and children are doing well," she enthused, as the man's balding head turned red.

"Aye, ma'am. My son works for 'is Grace and 'elps me in the stables. My wife passed last year," he said. "The ague."

Laying her gloved hand on the man's arm, she murmured, "I am very sorry for your loss, Frank."

Harriett's genuineness had been one of the things which had attracted Lucas, besides her many other more obvious, outward assets. "If you are ready to go, I see Frank has our mounts saddled," he interjected.

"Yes, Yer Grace. And Mrs. Nettles brung you a small basket for your outing," the man added. "I assumed you would ride Colton," he said.

"I will," Lucas replied.

Frank moved the mounting block to the horse and assisted Harriett onto her mount. It was good to see Frank's smile, even if it was over Lady Harriett Dudley. Losing his wife had been hard on the man. That she had asked most likely endeared her even more to him, Lucas thought. Was that jealousy he was feeling? *My God, I am jealous of an old man trying to help my guest onto her horse!*

"Your horse is beautiful," Harriett said, indicating the grey.

"Thank you. I should share the story of how I came to own him," he said, smiling at her, pleased to feel her attention on him. Lucas lashed the small hamper to the back of his saddle, securing it and marveling at Mrs. Nettles's clever choice of baskets. "Are you ready?" he asked, suddenly eager to get away from his stable.

She nodded, and they started slowly towards the back of his property.

As they passed his mother's orangery, he noticed the legs of a person standing under the branches of a tree near the door. Not able to make out who it was, he was tempted to circle back, but did not want to embarrass himself when it turned out to be a footman or kitchen person gathering items for dinner. He would ask Egerton to find out who it had been when he returned.

"I had forgotten you had an orangery," Harriett said, interrupting his reverie. "Mayhap we can visit it. It's been a while since I've had an orange as sweet as your gardener produces."

Her suggestion warmed Lucas and relaxed the coil of anxiety that had settled in his belly. They rode on in silence until he reached the stream that separated their properties. The rock rose into view, and he slowed Colton down. "Will this be all right with you?"

"I did not know where you might lead us, but this somehow seems àpropos," she supposed.

He slid down from his horse and tied Colton to the tree. Walking over to her, he lifted her down by her waist. "I am not sure what you mean by that," he said with a sigh. "We had many good memories from this spot, and I thought it might be a good one. But if you'd rather, we can move beyond."

His gaze locked with hers and at that moment, he could resist no more. He set her down in front of him and kissed her. When she did not resist, he increased the intensity of his kiss.

⤜⤜⤜✦⤛⤛⤛

HARRIETT FELT LOST and found at the same time. She wanted this kiss—she had dreamed of this kiss, *his kiss*. She lifted on her toes and curled her fingers in the nape of his hair. "Here. Stay here," she moaned in between breaths.

Lucas's arms drew her closer, and he dipped his head, peppering kisses on her neck, until he drew back. "I apologize, Harriett. I lost my head."

"Do you truly regret it?" she asked simply.

He studied her for a moment before answering. "No. I have wanted that kiss since I pulled you off your runaway horse. Perhaps I needed it for closure. But that is not why I brought you here."

Harriett felt conflicted. Her heart had never healed after Lucas. He had just made it clear the kiss was closure. And here they were, alone. Why had she agreed to this? She turned with her back to him, so he could not see her wipe away the tears that brimmed on her lower lid. "You asked me here to talk," she whispered hoarsely.

"I did." He gently turned her around, and with a finger, lifted her chin. "You've been crying."

"I was not crying. It was merely a speck of dirt in my eye from the ride. It is gone, now." She took a deep breath. "What did you have to ask me? I suppose you think I may know more than I told you."

He was silent before he began walking to the grey horse. "I brought some nourishment. Perhaps you will share some wine and cheese with me."

There was a slight breeze. She watched as he unfurled a red and white blanket and laid it down beside the high rock. He held out his hand and waited for her to take it. After a moment, she took his hand, relishing the warmth that sent familiar tingling heat through her. "I like your horse. He seems comfortable with you," she said, hoping to break the awkwardness that had become palpable since he broke their kiss.

He leaned back and looked at her. "I wanted to ask you some questions that I probably could have asked in your parlor. Except I wanted to have you away from any prying eyes or ears as we talked.

A shiver ran through her. Sitting on the blanket across from him, she appreciated his having chosen the side of the rock that shielded them from the wind. "I am here, now. What is it you want to know?" she asked.

His eyes narrowed. "I loved you, Harriett. You were to be my wife." he began. "Losing you was the hardest thing I have ever dealt with in my entire life."

"Why are you telling me this?" she asked, swiping at a tear. "Surely, you do not think I wanted to leave you. *I wrote to you, Lucas.* I begged you to come for me. I learned much later the three letters I wrote were never posted. Instead, my maid gave them to my husband, which earned me a beating. God only knows what it earned her," she said, as her breath came in gasps. Her chest heaved with the exertion of revealing what she had never revealed, even to her sister.

Lucas lifted her chin with his forefinger and leaned down and covered her trembling lips with his own.

This time, she broke the kiss. She pulled back and faced him, her chest still heaving. "Do not kiss me. I do not want your sympathy. I need only peace. I would never have broken your heart intentionally. I thought of all the things you once knew about me, that would have been foremost. Tell me what else you need to know, Your Grace, so I may return home, and we can be done with this."

His eyes became desolate as he looked at her. "I did not know. I sought only to understand why you never even told me of Dudley's death. I had to find out in the papers. I had foolishly expected to hear from you," he replied. "Never had I expected to see you again. And now, you have returned home . . ."

"Not for long. I have plans to leave soon," she lied. "I have received word of a property my solicitor assures me is perfect."

"You plan to leave . . . *when?*"

"I have a few commitments that I will see carried out, and then you will no longer be plagued by my existence."

He stood and walked to the stream's edge. "I had hoped . . ." he started but stopped.

"You hoped *what?*" Harriett said, standing. A knot formed in her throat as she stared at his back. She had known better than to agree to this. She should leave, but her feet remained planted where she stood.

He turned and gave a forced grin. "I apologize, Harriett. This is not going as I had anticipated. My hope was we could talk uninterrupted, and on our return, I would honor your earlier wish to visit the orangery. I recall it being your favorite treat."

The man was maddening. "Does that mean we are finished here?"

Lucas stepped closer, taking her hands "Do you want to leave?" He looked around. "We have history here," he said with a sly smile.

Harriett's tongue felt like it swelled in her throat. She opened her mouth to speak and closed it. Instead, she nodded. When he tugged her closer, she did not protest.

His warm lips covered hers in a light kiss. "I cannot seem to help myself. Tell me you want me to stop."

She did not want him to stop. She wanted him to want her . . . beyond the hugs and short kisses. She wanted him. Repeatedly, Lucas had made it clear he no longer wanted her in the forever sense, as he had once upon a time. Her lips opened slightly, and his tongue gained entry, softly probing her mouth. Its warmth ignited something deep within her core. Dudley had never been able to ignite as much as a candle in her presence. But with him, she felt there could be more, if only he wanted it. The heat in her belly alluded to more.

"Harriett," he started.

"Yes?" she asked, looking into his liquid brown eyes.

"Did you watch me? All those years ago," he whispered in her ear, sending shivers down her spine. "Were you here when I came out of the water . . . that day, long ago?"

Her heart beat a wild tattoo in her chest. *Where was this going?* "What do you want with me?" she panted. "Why are you asking me such a thing?"

"Why are you back?" he asked in a whisper.

She stepped back, her chest heaving. "I told you, Lucas," she panted. "Why are you confusing me? You say you have gotten over us, yet you kiss me. I am so confused."

"I do not know what came over me, Harriett," he entreated. "We should leave."

Confusion washed over her. "I agree. We should head back."

They rode in silence until the orangery was in view. Harriett noticed Lucas slowing his horse down. "I would understand if you do not want to stop. But allow me to pick up something," he said, sliding from his horse and tying it to a post in front of the building. He opened the door and disappeared inside.

He did not leave her much choice, she thought, watching him walk into the building. Oranges had always been a favorite treat of hers. Before she could change her mind, she slid out of her saddle and tied the mare next to the grey and followed Lucas into the building.

"What are you doing in here?" he asked, gathering a basket of oranges that had been placed on a table for him. "I had these gathered for you."

"This is special, Lucas," she said, taking the top orange and holding it. She relished the special fruit inside. "Thank you!"

"You are welcome," he said, placing his hand on her shoulder and squeezing it lightly.

It had always been a sign of his affection, years ago, she recalled, realizing it only added to her confusion where the duke was concerned. The sooner she left, the better things would be for her. At least, then, she could establish what normal would be for her. Here, she felt like she was caught between the life she knew five years past, and the one punctuated by her husband's untimely death.

As they approached the door, a loud lock sounded from the outside.

Lucas pulled on the handle, trying to free it.

"Are we locked in here?" Harriett asked in a panicked voice.

Lucas rattled the door again, shaking it. "The lock outside came down on its own, I suspect. I had asked that it be repaired, but it appears it was not. We may have to wait a little while," he said.

CHAPTER FIFTEEN

F EAR CLUTCHED AT her heart. Harriett hated enclosed spaces. Dudley would lock her in her room when she disobeyed him. With the windows locked, she could do nothing but sit there and panic. How was she locked in the orangery with Lucas, of all people? "What do we do now?" She took a big gulping breath and exhaled slowly. "Lucas, is there a back way out?"

"Harriett, what is wrong?" He rushed to her and pulled her close. "You may not believe me, but I do not know how we came to be locked in here. If it were the greenhouse, we would have tools and a key." He stopped talking and walked to the door, feeling around the upper edge. "I had asked for a key to be placed up here, to prevent being locked in, but," he grunted as he moved his hand across. "There does not appear to be one." He felt over the transom again, brushing off the top and pulling back. "Ouch!"

His sharp outcry of pain riveted her attention. "Are you hurt?" She rushed back to him and saw the blood running down his arm.

"It is just a slight cut. I think I snagged it on a splinter," he admitted.

"Then we need to clean it. The windows are fogged with moisture. Perhaps that would help," Harriett said, ripping off a piece of her petticoat, and wiping a corner of the window. Taking his hand, she dabbed at the blood, cleaning the cut. "I can see the splinter," she said, tugging his arm gently towards the light. "This may hurt a little. I want to squeeze this and force the splinter to the surface of the skin."

"You are no longer panicking, Harriett," he observed, touching her arm. "Perhaps focusing on something other than the isolation helps."

Her skin quivered from his touch, and she looked up and smiled. "My breathing has slowed," she acknowledged. "All these years, I have never been successful in stopping the panic."

He took his hand away and cradled her face. "What do you mean by that? Does this happen often?"

Harriett looked away. "It used to, a lot. Dudley would lock me in my room when I displeased him."

"Your window?"

"He nailed my windows shut. The day he found my notes to you, his displeasure knew no bounds. He beat me and then locked me in my room," she replied.

Lucas's face reddened in anger. "The man deserved the end he met," he seethed. "You mentioned his anger before, at High Rock." He took a deep breath and gave a shuddering exhale. "I tried to find you, Harriett. My heart shattered when you left. Mayhap I should have done more to find you, but your parents said you married another. They refused to speak to me. I had to force what I could from your father. Even my father tried to find you, but there was nothing to be done. At first, he refused to tell me where he found you, fearing I would do something crazy like kidnap you or challenge the man."

"You would have come for me even though you knew I had married?" she asked, meeting his gaze.

He nodded. "My father forbade me to go. We argued, but he gradually made me see the futility of it, even though the pain hurt worse than anything a battlefield could have inflicted."

The old duke had been like another father to her. While not surprised to hear his father had searched for her, it stirred her heart and moved her to tears. "Oh, Lucas," she said, touching his face tenderly. "I felt the same pain. And I still do not know why Father forced me to marry Lord Dudley. There was nothing to be done. My husband surrounded me with servants loyal only to him. I had no friends." A tear trailed down her face, and she took another gulping breath. She felt the staccato of her heartbeat increase. "I did what they required, but I was not sad the day he died," she admitted, leaning into his chest.

She lifted her head, sniffled, and swiped at the tears. "I must find my way out of here, or I fear the panic will return. But first, we should take care of this splinter. I see it sticking out. It could become infected." Using her nails together, she attempted to grip the splinter over and over, until she finally felt it between her fingers and pulled softly, extracting a half-inch, bloodied splinter. "This will hurt," she said, squeezing the finger to make it bleed. "But it flushes out the poisons and dirt. At least that is what I have been told."

When she looked up at his face, she noticed she Lucas's face seemed transfixed upon hers.

"Thank you, Harriett. I felt relief as soon as you extracted it." He took her face in his palms again. "Never has a more beautiful nurse assisted me in my hour of need." Lucas pulled her closer. "I can no longer fight the urge to kiss your luscious pink lips." He leaned down and covered her lips with his.

Harriett became immersed in the kiss until she remembered his terse pledge to remain unattached. Harriett pushed back on him, her chest heaving. "Lucas, please do not toy with me. I could not take losing you a second time."

He drew back, seeming to stiffen at her words. Moving to the same window she had used to gather moisture, he put his palms on the sill and leaned his head against the glass. "I am truly sorry, Harriett. I would never intentionally hurt you. And that seems all I have done. I took you out today to speak with you. Why did you not write to me when Dudley died?" His voice sounded pained, even to himself. "I discovered his passing through the papers, and I waited . . . It was a fresh wave of agony to wade through. A rejection—which hurt as much as when you left."

That explains some of why he was so opposed to her openly. But not all. "*Why* are you kissing me?" she demanded, her voice low. "I did not reject you."

Without turning to face her, he replied. "Forgive my inability to keep my hands to myself. I want you, Harriett," he said, standing up and turning around. "I do not know how I feel about everything else, including marriage, except that I want you."

Without saying a word, she rose on her toes and kissed him. "I cannot be one of those women—the widows that find pleasure where they want it," she said evenly.

"My life has snowballed, it seems," he said, reaching for an orange from the basket sitting near him. He held the fruit and stared at it. "I have two young women I am responsible for—one that challenges all tenets of good behavior. Both are in mourning over their parents, whom I can barely recall. My mother has organized some sort of . . . I am not sure what she has organized," he said, shaking his head. "But she invited you here . . . you, whom I had thought to have resolved all my feelings for but once again, find my heart and mind in constant conflict. I find myself unable to wrap my head around it all, despite my best efforts." His fingers sought hers and curled around her hands.

"When you put it like that, I suppose I understand the up-heaval in your life. Your brothers . . . they are back at school, at least," she said with a slight laugh.

"They are," he smiled. "At least that part of life seems in order. You realize my moniker among my friends is the 'Duke of Disorder' and what I have just described is my life—something so disorganized anyone would think I made it up. Except it's all true," he said with a shy grin. "I suppose it is *why* my friends have always called me such. I have a penchant for making a muck of things."

"The nickname fits, but not always," she giggled. "You forgot to mention you have added a spirited steed to your stables intending to race."

"I forgot that." He craned his neck to the window and looked outside. "The horses are still out there. Perhaps someone will see them. I would hate for them to think the worst of us . . . and label you one of *those* widows." He gave a sly grin.

Despite herself, she enjoyed the way he playfully tossed her words back at her. But she knew he had gotten the message. Harriett wrapped her arms about her shoulders to quell a shiver. A sense of panic lay just below the surface, even though being trapped here with Lucas had been different. His presence had stayed that feeling of isolation. He made her feel . . . wanted. She wished she could have said loved. But that was not to be. They had had their chance. She had heard what he had to say and better understood his struggle.

"Lucas, his heir has contacted me. I do not understand what he wants of me, but I cannot possibly go back there. I will not. For that reason, I am leaving soon. I must find peace somewhere. It cannot be with my parents. Father acts peculiarly around me. And I feel my presence has further strained their relationship. I must leave."

"I can contact the viscount and find out what he wants," he offered.

"No, I do not want you to get involved. Please promise me you will not. I only wished to explain why I was leaving," Harriett replied, casting her eyes away from his. "I understand all you said a few minutes ago. There is no future for us. Our chance has passed."

He became silent for several long moments until finally, he spoke. "I was being honest about still wanting you."

"I know. And I was being equally honest about not being able to play the part of the loose widow," she answered.

"My God! I have been a cad," he whispered, anguish clear in his voice.

"No! You have done no such thing. We still have a powerful attraction to each other. However, you have explained things, and so have I. We needed to clear the air. I will carry out my promise to your mother, and then I will leave," she said. *Except, I feel much more than attraction*, she thought in anguish.

"And your promise is . . ." he said, waiting.

"To teach the girls painting—or at least assess their abilities," she rejoined.

"Lucas, are you in there?"

It was his friend, Lord Romney's voice.

"Yes, Romney, I am here with Lady Dudley. Somehow, the door locked us in . . ."

The door opened, cutting him off.

"How did you find us? No—thank you for finding us!" Lucas said, picking up the basket of oranges. "I came in to get this basket, and Lady Dudley followed. The door closed behind us. I had ordered a key kept here, but it was gone, as well."

The man stood there in front of them, arms akimbo, grinning. "I wager you have not suffered."

"How did you know I was in here?" Lucas persisted with a snarl.

Lord Romney remained silent. "It would be better to move past this and let it go," he finally said.

Lucas glared at his friend, but Lord Romney made it clear he was not telling. His gaze swept over her as he uttered some words to Lucas that she could not hear. Harriett could not imagine its import. At this moment, all she cared about was being free of the locked room and the ensuing panic. Even if it meant the time alone with Lucas had ended. Her relief was palpable. She stepped to the door and inhaled the crisp air. Memories of being locked in her room in Kent were too fresh and served as a reminder that her panic could have made their unexpected confinement together much worse.

CHAPTER SIXTEEN

The next day

HARRIETT ARRIVED AT Pembley Manor at the agreed-upon time of ten of the clock. She felt exhausted, having tossed, turned, and cried in whatever sleep she had gained. Once her maid saw the deep circles beneath Harriett's eyes and the red puffiness above them, Jane had been insistent that Harriett allow her to use a small jade roller to refresh her face. It was a beauty trick Harriett had observed her grandmother use. Once she told Jane about it, the maid had secured a small roller and often integrated it into her morning and evening routine, something Harriett enjoyed.

Her footman followed her up the steps of the manor, carrying the package of paints, canvases, and her easel.

"Lady Dudley, Her Grace is expecting you in the parlor," Egerton said, opening the door.

"Thank you," she said, handing him her pelisse and gloves. "Timmons has my supplies."

The butler snapped his fingers, and another footman relieved Timmons of the materials and followed Harriett to the parlor, where the butler announced her arrival.

"Lady Dudley, thank you for coming today. You have a love-ly day for your painting lesson, and the girls are most excited," the duchess gushed, walking to greet Harriett.

"I have been looking forward to this. After hearing your young ladies express a desire to paint more than landscapes, I have been eager to see what they produce," Harriett replied. She was anxious to finish with the day and hoped it would be without running into Lucas.

"It was extremely nice of you to bring the paints and canvas. I confess to having forgotten to requisition them from town," Her Grace said. "The girls have been told to meet you in the solarium, upstairs."

The sooner she met with the girls, the sooner she could leave. The thought of a nap when she returned home sustained her. Harriett hoped she would not fall asleep standing behind her easel. As she approached the landing on the second floor, she heard the footsteps coming down from the upper floor. It had to be Lucas. Determined not to run into him, Harriett picked up her speed and quickly stepped onto the floor, quickening her steps until she reached the solarium. She listened for the footfalls, but they had halted. Yesterday had been an exceptionally hard day, one that she hoped *not* to repeat today.

"Lady Dudley," his voice called from behind her.

Drat! She stopped and whirled to face him, forcing a smile. "Your Grace. How nice to see you this fine morning."

"It is an unexpected pleasure to see you as well. Welcome."

Harriett's gaze locked with his, each appearing to read the other's thoughts. After a moment, Harriett blinked and glanced down before looking at him. "Thank you, Your Grace. I am here to conduct the painting lessons for Ladies Beatrice and Catherine."

He dipped his head in a polite nod. "In that case, I will escort you to the conservatory where the ladies await."

Her neck and face flushed with heat, and she fought the impulse to fan herself. It had probably been foolish to think she could evade Lucas's presence in his own house. "Thank you. I know the way and am heading there, now." Her tone was abrupt.

"Are you well today, Harriett?" he asked, making her stop again.

"Of course, Your... Lucas. Perhaps I need more rest. I did not sleep well last night." She refused to look at him, realizing he would naturally assume it had something to do with him.

"Mayhap rest would make a difference. I apologize for my part in that. I did not know the lock would malfunction," Lucas proffered.

"Do you truly believe that occurred?" she murmured. Her gut told her it had been intentional, but *not* by Lucas. What would anyone have to gain by locking the two of them in the orangery? Her reputation as a widow was not as fragile as that of a debutante and their discovery together by someone other than a friend would not have produced a forced marriage.

The very word *marriage* forced a shudder. She never planned to marry again.

"Do you think Lord Romney knows?" she asked. It had seemed he might.

"He will not say. I have my suspicions; however, it would be hard to prove," he answered.

His answer gave her a start, but she schooled her face. "I should get in there with the girls. I appreciated your candor yesterday," she said.

The door to the room closed behind her and she pasted a smile on her face, before walking toward the duchess and her two charges.

"Welcome, Lady Dudley. This room has excellent light, do you agree?" Her Grace asked, walking toward her. "I used to paint in this room and always enjoyed it. The girls should be able to produce their best work in here."

The loud meow of a cat sounded, drawing everyone's attention to the covered basket near Cat. The lid pushed up, and a small, furry head popped out.

Harriet noticed the duchess's facial expression change from surprise to irritation and back to surprise. She bit her tongue to keep from laughing. *Cat wanted to paint her kitten. I guess she meant it.* "You both mentioned wanting to paint animals, and I thought we could do that today."

"I would like to paint Greyson," Cat stated stubbornly, pulling the purring animal out of the basket, and placing him on her lap. The cat remained still as if it knew it was important.

"Lady Catherine, that sounds like a fine idea. Look what a patient subject he is," Harriett soothed. She turned to the older sister. "Lady Beatrice, what would you enjoy painting?"

"Mama had a beautiful necklace. We could not find it after she died," she replied sadly.

"Can you describe it?" Harriett asked, unsure why she asked such a thing.

"I believe I recall seeing your mother in a stunning sapphire necklace when I first met her," the duchess offered.

"That is the one, Your Grace," Beatrice agreed, looking downcast. "I cannot imagine what happened to it when they died. My mother told me once it had been her own mother's. I thought painting it might make her seem closer."

Lady Beatrice's words reminded Harriett of the sorrow these girls still felt and chastised her own pretense at mourning a husband she did not care for nor appreciate. He had robbed her of a life of love.

"Lady Catherine, have you been instructed on painting animals?" she asked, stepping closer to the younger girl.

"Mama taught us to paint," Beatrice volunteered. Her voice sounded pained. "She loved to paint."

"She taught us that the canvas should tell a story," added Lady Catherine.

"Did she teach you to paint from memory?" Harriett asked Lady Beatrice.

"Yes. That was the way we painted," the older girl replied.

"Perhaps we can begin. Your Grace, will you be joining us?" Harriett asked.

"I would enjoy that," the duchess said, ringing a bell. Two

footmen entered, carrying easels, canvases, and paints, setting them up along the windows. "Ladies, the easels are of various sizes and heights. Sometimes I sit and paint. Use any easel you want," the duchess said, taking the one closest to her and pulling up a chair.

For the next several hours, Greyson's rare protestations and their brushes flowing against the canvases were the only sounds heard.

Harriett peered over the top of her easel and felt an overwhelming urge to look. Putting down her brush, she walked past Lady Catherine's easel. Cat had painted a grey horse that looked remarkably like Lucas's. Momentarily, she wondered when the girl had seen the horse. Perhaps she had gone to the stables to look, she thought. Greyson had emerged on the canvas in perfect form. "You paint beautifully, Lady Catherine! The representation looks like he could step off the page and meow! Why did you choose to paint Luc ... er ... the duke's new horse with the kitten?"

"It was something His Grace told me after I adopted Greyson from the barn," she said with a sly smile. "His Grace told me cats calm horses. Neither one threatens the other, making them perfect together."

Enthused, Harriett moved to Lady Beatrice's easel. The older sister had painted what Harriett assumed was a cameo of her mother, wearing a stunning sapphire and diamond necklace. "Your mother was beautiful. I can see bits of both you and your sister in her face. And her necklace is lovely. You have tremendous talent—esteem for your dear mother."

She went no further than Lady Beatrice's canvas, preferring to not place herself in an awkward position with Her Grace. "I am pleased with these efforts," she said enthusiastically. "I am almost certain either of you ladies could give me lessons!"

The duchess put her paintbrush down and peered across the top of her easel. "I must see!" she said, quickly wiping her hands and moving around the room, first to Lady Catherine and then to

Lady Beatrice. "These are wonderful, ladies!" she said, clapping her hands in glee. She looked at Harriett. "Would you be able to continue with us for a few days before you leave?"

"You plan to leave?" Lady Catherine said as she stuck her brush in the water.

Harriett placed her brush in the water and stepped back, surprised by the emotion expressed by the younger sister. "I have always been planning to leave, Cat. I spent the last year in mourning and came to see my family, whom I had not seen in five years."

"Where will you go?" Cat asked while she continued to paint.

Harriett smiled. "My solicitor seeks to find a small country home for me to purchase. I would look myself, but society makes it difficult for women to make purchases. For the time being, I planned to move to London to the townhouse I inherited."

"Can we come and see you?" Cat asked in a trembly voice.

Harriett felt confused. "Of course you can. Her Grace plans a trip to London for your sister's Season. I will make it a point to spend time together."

"I . . . thought you would be here longer," Cat replied meekly.

A laugh bubbled up in Harriett's throat, and she squashed it. After being locked in a greenhouse with him yesterday, she was almost certain she had worn out her welcome with Lucas. *Why would Cat think she would be here longer? Strange.*

"Let us see what you have captured," said the duchess, stepping up behind her. "Why, it is a beautiful depiction of the orangery. I have always loved the details of the architecture, and you have captured it perfectly." The matron stepped back and clasped her hands excitedly.

Harriett walked back to her easel, unsure of what to say. She had been so lost in her thoughts as they painted; she had not realized she had painted the object of her musings. *How in the world do I explain this painting?*

"What has excited you so, Mother?" Lucas said, walking into

the room and stopping next to his mother. "You captured the details brilliantly, Lady Dudley."

He stood close enough that she could hear the slight intake of his breath when he saw her painting. Heat prickled her neck when he lifted his gaze from the canvas to her face, gazing at her with a knowing grin.

CHAPTER SEVENTEEN

The next day

"I UNDERSTAND YOU and Lady Dudley picked oranges yesterday, together," teased Clarendon as he stacked his breakfast plate. Putting down the serving spoon, he turned and held a seat open for his wife, who was right behind him, then sat next to her.

Lucas folded his newspaper and placed it next to his serviette. "Very cute!"

At the remarks, his mother lifted her head and smiled. "Darling, don't be so sensitive."

"We had gone inside to look around and pick up something I had asked the staff to prepare. Within minutes, the door closed and abruptly locked us inside the orangery. I am afraid we forgot them in our haste to leave once Romney opened the door. Perhaps one of you saw something." He glanced around at blank expressions. "Anything?" Someone had to know something, he reasoned to himself.

"I am afraid the girls and I were upstairs in the solarium with Lady Penfield," the duchess said blithely, picking up her serviette and shaking it before laying it into her lap.

"Lady Penfield was here? I did not realize," Lucas said dismissively, buttering his toast.

"She arrived an hour after you left with Lady Dudley," his mother said.

"When did you and Lady Penfield become friends?" he asked. "I never recall her being a visitor before."

"Lucas, do not be silly. I have lots of friends," his mother chastised.

He noticed Romney's arched brow, but the man did not say a word.

Deciding to prod and discover what the man knew, Lucas turned to thank him, lifting his buttered toast in a vague salute. "We appreciated your rescue. Never had I ever imagined getting locked in the orangery. Harriett . . . Lady Dudley and I stopped to retrieve a basket of oranges my staff had gathered. Oranges have always been her favorite, and I wanted to surprise her." Lucas was unsure why he felt compelled to add that last bit. A vision of her with a quarter orange rind in her mouth covering her teeth made him smile. They had been frequent visitors to the green-house before she had left him. He turned his attention to his mother, who at that moment was in an animated discussion with Lady Clarendon and Lady Romney at the lower end of the table. "Mother, what plans do you have for the day?"

Lucas's mother glanced in his direction before turning her attention to her tea. "That was very kind to think of the oranges. I had forgotten Lady Dudley enjoyed them. The countess has been doing a favor for us . . . me, I suppose . . . in helping the girls. I could have gotten her a basket, as well." She shook her head as if to clear it. "To answer your question, Lady Wilton invited me for tea today. The ladies Clarendon and Romney have agreed to attend with me," she drawled.

He nodded. He had purposely kept his plans for the day loose, hoping to smooth things over with Harriett. Still angry about becoming locked in the orangery, he felt a level of urgency to resolve the mystery of how it happened. *Hell's teeth! A door does not just lock itself.* It would take time, but he would understand the disaster. And a disaster was precisely how he regarded it.

"Do you feel up to riding today?" Romney asked.

"The weather is crisp and dry. It is a perfect day to take Colton out," added Clarendon. "I am itching to ride him."

"Please be careful, dear," Lady Clarendon interjected. "A broken bone could severely limit your activities for the upcoming holidays, not to mention provide a memorable discussion point for the portrait we are having painted."

"You have nothing to worry about, Charlotte. I promise to come back in one piece," Clarendon said, bantering good-naturedly with his wife.

"We have my wife, who brought me back to life," Romney said, chuckling. "But I am not sure even she can urge a broken bone to mend quickly."

"You give me too much credit, darling. I did not bring you back to life. However, seeing that handsome face of yours, I tried my best to save your life," returned Lady Romney. "Let us hope you men do nothing that requires stitches or mending."

"Sounds ideal," Lucas agreed. "As soon as breakfast ends, we can head out." Turning to Trask, who stood near the door, he ordered Dirk, Colton, and the steed Romney favored saddled and brought round. Finishing his meal, he contemplated the events of the day before, yet each time he thought about it, his gut told him Romney knew something. However, his dear friend refused to say a word. Romney would say nothing that could aggravate a problem, and certainly, when Lucas found out who did it, there would be a problem. However, he was uncertain that this predicament could get any worse. Harriett would leave soon, and he had still not reconciled the whole nasty situation. No matter, he planned to avoid marriage at any cost. She did not seem of the same accord. This should no longer bother him, yet it did.

"Ladies, please do not leave the table on my account," the duchess said, standing. "I must check in with the girls before we leave. Tea is at noon, so we have plenty of time. I shall meet you in the front parlor." With that, his mother left the room, sweeping out of the door just before Trask returned.

"The horses will be ready shortly, Your Grace," the footman said.

"Thank you, Trask," Lucas replied. "There is one more thing. I am sorry to have forgotten it with my original request, but here is what I would like done. Please step out here with me while everyone finishes their meal."

In less than thirty minutes, all three men rode in the stream's direction that joined his property with the Earl of Scarsdale's lands. Lucas decided not to explain his choice of direction. It would soon become obvious.

"Colton seems to have gotten much more accustomed to being ridden," Clarendon said, breaking a long silence.

"I had noticed that myself." Lucas nodded. "I hope he will be ready for the Spring races."

"Do you have a lead on a jockey?" Clarendon asked.

"Mr. Frank's son, Jeremy, has expressed interest. Frank says he has been riding some races. I am having his experience verified, while I have no reason not to believe Frank."

"You are smart to do that, Dorman. If people bet on the man and lose, then find out later he misrepresented his experience, it could present a problem," agreed Romney. "It's an unforgiving problem and one best avoided."

"I agree. Not meaning to change the subject, but have you had any luck finding your horse?"

"Sadly, no. The enemy shot me while riding, and Sable cried out, but other than commanding her to run, I recall nothing more," Romney said, clearing his throat to hide the emotion, but Lucas could still hear it in his friend's voice.

The animal had almost been a lifelong pet, and Romney realized he had risked the mare's life by taking her across the ocean to war, even if that war was one no one believed would last. "I apologize for bringing that up, Romney. Forgive me."

"No, no. It is fine. I have adjusted. When I could have looked for Sable, I was unable. Blind men have a hard time searching," he said with a strained look. "I only hope that wherever Sable is, they have given her proper care. It is all I can ask."

"I remember this place!" Clarendon said as they moved into the clearing near the water's edge. Several evergreens framed the area, while other hardwoods had lost their leaves. Clarendon slid from Colton's saddle and walked to the large rock in the center of the clearing. "The high rock! You have a penchant for this place it seems," Clarendon chortled.

"It holds many memories for me—all of them special, and most of them with you fellows," Lucas explained.

"Are we here to create another memory?" Romney asked, jesting.

"Perhaps," Lucas replied.

"You said it would be too cold to swim," Clarendon hooted. "Have you changed your mind? I will race you."

"The water *is* too cold. I have no intention of swimming," Lucas returned. The sounds of a horse coming silenced the three men. Lucas stared in the sound's direction, a slight smile forming on his lips.

A smallish man that Lucas did not recognize rode into the clearing. His immediate thought was frustration. He had not thought to bring a weapon. However, the diminutive size of the rider made it feel unnecessary.

"My name is Jeremy Frank, Your Grace," the rider said as he rode up upon a black mare with white feet and a white bib. A white spot tipped her right ear.

Romney turned to Lucas, swiping at tears. "I do not deserve friends like the two of you," he said, sliding from the steed he had ridden to the clearing. He walked up to Lucas and reached up for his hand, grasping it before squeezing his friend to his chest. "Thank you, my friend."

"I was wondering when Sable would show herself," Clarendon whispered under his breath to Lucas.

Romney gave the steed's reins to the stablehand and took his horse, burying his face in her chest. "I do not know where or how you came to find her. Except for my family, this is the greatest gift anyone has ever given me. I cannot wait to introduce her to Bethany."

"She is eager to hear from you and wants to see you ride her," Clarendon assured his friend, swiping at his own eyes. "My God! You'd think she belonged to all of us."

"He's right," Lucas said. "The three of us used every connection we had to find her. She was supposed to arrive here two weeks ago, but the ship she was on from Scotland met with delays."

"Scotland?" Romney questioned.

"Yes. The war horse had been 'adopted' by another officer, a Scot. Once we were corresponding with him and explained your story, he would hear of nothing but returning her to you. We could have had her ridden here but did not wish to risk injury," Lucas explained. "We were getting worried you would want to leave before she arrived. And we wanted to surprise you."

"Neighhhhh!" Sable brayed, nuzzling Romney's neck.

"I never thought to see her again. I had tried to find her myself. But to no avail," Romney said haltingly in a choked voice.

"Indeed! We told them to add that search to ours," Clarendon said with a laugh.

"Bethany knows?" Romney asked, his voice one of disbelief.

"Yes, and she cannot wait to see you. The tea Mother spoke of never existed. It was a ruse to get you out here with us. Banbury had much to do with this, I should add. He hated not to see you and your pet reunited, but his wife would probably never have understood his reluctance to travel with her following their wedding," Lucas said, grinning. He looked over at the stablehand, who stood silently, now holding the steed. "Did you say your name was Jeremy? Jeremy Frank?"

"I did. Pa thought it a good way to meet you, Your Grace. If you do not agree, please do not be angry with him," Frank replied.

"Surprises abound all the way around!" exclaimed Clarendon. "Shall I let you ride Colton and see how it goes?"

"A brilliant idea!" agreed Romney, trying to mount his horse, whose excitement was palpable to everyone there.

"Judging from the look in his eyes, I would say this steed has a lot to offer," Frank replied. He lifted himself onto Colton's saddle and got comfortable.

"Shall we ride?" Clarendon suggested.

"Neighhhhh!" Sable whinnied, happily scratching her feet into the ground.

"I think she is eager for you to ride her, my friend," Lucas added.

"My heart is full," Romney said, leaning down and hugging his horse. "I've missed her so much and can never thank the three of you enough."

"It thrills all of us to see you with your sweet Sable again. I will write Banbury and let him know," Lucas offered.

"No. Allow me to do that. I owe each of you a great debt. You never gave up on me, and it appears you did not give up on Sable, either. It was my lucky day when we three became brothers at heart," Romney replied, his voice full of emotion.

"It was lucky for all of us!" Clarendon corrected.

"Hear, hear!" Lucas cheered, urging Dirk ahead. "Let us ride. I need to see what Frank can do with Colton here."

As the three friends crested the first hill, a grey horse blew past them with ease.

"Let's catch them," Romney said, squeezing Sable's flanks.

CHAPTER EIGHTEEN

"**I** SEE HORSES coming," called Cat, who had been designated the official lookout. "Although, they are still some distance away."

"Are you sure they will want me to be here?" questioned Harriett, unsure her sister and the duchess had not talked her into something she was going to regret. She was not part of his family.

"Certainly, they will," Lady Romney interjected. "Matthew lost so much over there. I am glad they found Sable."

"He also gained so much," emphasized the duchess. "He was always different from the others—much more invested in the little things."

"He was, indeed. And my little brother has somehow become much the same," lamented Lady Clarendon. "We sorely missed my brother when my father died. It was hard on our mother. But then, he arrived home with a sister in tow and now a child. We are blessed. It seems fitting that Sable returns, too . . . and so lucky."

"Here they come!" Cat shouted.

"Shhh!" her sister admonished under her breath.

"Let's meet them outside," suggested the duchess. "Stay on, Harriett. You are part of the celebration."

Despite the invitation, Harriett felt out of place. She wanted to say that but could not bring herself to do anything but follow along.

"Can you believe they found the horse?" Cat asked Harriett, coming up beside her. "What are the possibilities?"

"Indeed," agreed Lady Alice Penfield, leaving the parlor with her skirts swishing about her.

"I did not realize you planned to join us," her sister said.

"I had not planned. Rather, I think something is happening at home that you need to be aware of. So, I came to warn you . . . or gather you home, should you think either more appropriate."

"Why? What has happened?" Harriett said, nervously nibbling her lower lip.

Alice hugged her sister. "Perhaps we can speak of it when we have a moment alone. I cannot make sense of it. A man came to the house to deliver a message to you. Father intercepted it, according to Nichols. He described Father as rattled and upset."

Seeing no time they could steal away, Harriett tugged on Alice's sleeve, signaling her to stay behind with her. The two women moved off to the side as Lady Beatrice joined the other women. "I cannot imagine what it could be about," Harriett said, suddenly no longer wanting to leave Pembley Manor, when, only five minutes prior, she had.

"Father's behavior has been curious ever since he sent you off with Dudley," Alice added. "Still, I hate to see him this way. When I saw him, he was shaking, and he told Mama he may have to leave."

"That certainly sounds strange, but I am realistic enough to know my presence upsets him further. There is little I can do to help him. He never speaks to me." It was a difficult predicament. She loved her father, but the closeness they had once shared no longer existed. She did not know what could have upset her father, given the message was for her. That was another reason she needed to leave. Her father insisted on reading her missives, according to Jane. She discovered it when Jane gave her some opened correspondence. "I hope it was from the milliner or someone I am expecting."

"You mentioned Lord Dudley's heir had asked you to meet him. Do you think he would pursue you?" Alice whispered.

"I do not know." Harriett wanted nothing to do with that family. Never again. His mother had hurled insane remarks and threats her way when Dudley had bequeathed the property to her, decrying the unfairness of it. *"You bewitched him somehow. The Viscount will see you will have nothing. You hear me?"* the old woman had screamed the last time she saw her.

Yet, the new Viscount Dudley had not spoken more than a few words to her—not even enough for her to form an opinion of the man. If the message was again from him, what did he want of her? What could the man possibly need? If he was anything like Dudley, perhaps he envisioned gaining the rest of her dowry—the money Dudley's solicitor said her husband had placed in an account with her name on it. It was a large sum of money and very uncharacteristic of Dudley to give her any money. Pin money had been almost nonexistent in her entire marriage. Everything had to be approved for purchase by either Dudley or his mother. Even in her name, the account would have been her husband's by law. Had Dudley been trying to hide the money? "Maybe the new viscount intends to fight the will and make me go back," she speculated loud enough for Alice to hear. "I have just gotten away from Kent. I refuse to return."

"Father would not allow . . ." Alice started but stopped in the middle of the sentence.

"I see them. The men are almost here!" squealed Cat from the portico just beyond them. It had thrilled Cat to learn of the war horse's rescue, and she had peppered them with questions this morning, once Lord Clarendon and Lucas had informed them of the plans to reunite the horse and Lord Romney. It was a very generous gift, making Harriett feel slightly envious. No one in her life would go to that level of trouble for her, except perhaps her sister.

The duchess had developed her ruse to leave the men alone. Cat wanted to be there for the revelation, but her sister kept a tight watch on her, fearful of what might happen if she continued to disappoint the duke—even though he had assured them this was their home. According to Lady Clarendon, they planned to surprise him at a place that had meant a lot to all of them growing up. Harriett knew it was High Rock but refused to elaborate when asked about it.

She tugged her sister's arm, and the two rejoined the other ladies. *Lucas sits in fine form on a horse*, Harriett thought, watching the men crest the small hill together. She noticed Colton was not with them and assumed a stablehand had returned him to the barn.

"Look at my husband. I can see his smile from here. This surprise was such a nice thing to do," Lady Romney said excitedly.

"They act as if they have never been apart," observed the duchess.

"They are not apart in their hearts. My husband swears he heard them speak to him while lying on the battlefield, encouraging him and telling him not to give up. I am not sure I would have found him alive had they not been with him in spirit," Lady Romney added.

"That gives me chills," Harriett said, giving an affectionate hug to the countess. "I am glad you found him."

"That horse is a beauty!" exclaimed Cat.

"Meow," echoed Greyson, who protested his position under her arm.

"Do not start any mischief, Lady Catherine," warned the duchess under her breath. But they all heard it.

As soon as the men dismounted and handed the horses to the waiting stablehands, Cat led the ladies outside to see the horse and congratulate Lord Romney.

"Did you see what my best friends did for me, darling?" Lord Romney said, greeting his wife with a hug.

"I cannot believe they found her," his wife said. The other women echoed her remarks.

Harriett pasted a smile on her face. She was happy for Lord Romney, but she needed to leave. Her sister's news overtook her thoughts. "Alice, you were right. We need to leave. Let me say my goodbyes to the duchess and the other ladies."

"You are leaving?" Lucas asked, up beside her.

Startled, Harriett spun to face the duke. "I am sorry, yes. My father intercepted a message that upset him. I must get home."

"Would it help for me to come with you?" he asked.

Her heart cried out *yes* as she shook her head. "No. I appreciate your offer. If I need anything, I can reach out."

"I understand. Perhaps I overstepped," Lucas offered.

"No. My answer came out a bit rushed. I am not sure what I will find out," she admitted. "Alice said whatever he intercepted has rattled our father."

"That's odd, indeed. You mentioned that Dudley's heir had reached out to you. Do you believe this is connected?"

"I don't know. But I must leave," Harriett said, giving a slight curtsey.

LUCAS WATCHED HARRIETT and her sister leave but could not be sure she was leaving for the reasons she gave. He had not known she would be at the house, but when he saw her, he had hoped to have time to apologize for yesterday. But not with his mother and friends watching.

Being locked in the orangery with her made him realize how much he had missed her. Unfortunately, they may have lost their chance to change that.

"You have that look about you," Romney said, walking up and handing him a drink. "The look like you are wading through a problem, knee-deep in it."

"I have always been transparent to you three," he said, referring to his friends.

Romney nodded. "You are going to let her leave without clearing things up from yesterday?"

"You could help that if you told me what you know," Lucas said guardedly.

"Ah," Romney said, sipping his drink. "So, that is the price," he joked. "I know nothing more than I told you yesterday."

"There it is—the look that tells me I am going to lose this argument," laughed Lucas. "And there is no price. I just thought you might have seen who locked us in the building." He would have to figure out who locked them in the orangery without Romney's help. He took a sip of his drink. "You suspected nothing . . . about Sable, that is?" he asked his friend.

"No! You had me on that one. I am so happy to have Sable back. I appreciate everything you did to get her for me. I've had her since I was fifteen. I thought had I lost her and cursed myself countless times for taking her across the ocean and not leaving her with my family."

"You are our friend. We were determined to turn over every rock we could to find her. And we did!" Lucas extended his hand to Romney, who took it and pulled him close for a hug.

"'Thank you' seems too little," Romney said.

Clarendon hugged him. "We are all so pleased."

"If you boys have finally finished with hugging and congratulating each other, we would like to celebrate . . . not only your horse, Lord Romney, but having you all here with us today," the duchess said dryly.

"I find I am hungry, Your Grace," Clarendon said, wearing a sly grin. "Let us head to the dining room and celebrate!"

Lucas shrugged off the irritation he felt with his mother's interruption and went along with her. He had noticed his mother's demeanor became slightly testy when Harriett and her sister left. Perhaps part of his mother's annoyance was with Cat, who was clamoring to get to know Sable, Romney's horse. Did she just ask him to let her ride the beast? Of course, Romney would not allow it, but his mother would surely have heard the request. Poor girl.

"Lady Catherine, do you have a few minutes?" he asked above the raucous congratulatory laughter and conversation with Romney and his wife.

"Yes, Your Grace," the girl replied, picking up Greyson and leaving Sable's side.

Lucas noticed her older sister looking sharply at her. "Walk with me," he said, leading his young ward to his office.

She held the kitten close as they walked into his office. "Have a seat, Lady Catherine," he suggested, wearing a grin.

"Mew!" the kitten protested as they entered.

"This sounds serious," the girl said, sitting down. "Greyson, you are not in trouble, little fellow." She scratched him behind the ears to calm him.

"Ha! No, he is not in trouble. Are you enjoying yourself?" he asked, taking a seat.

"I am, Your Grace. Very much." She looked around the room. "You have a lot of books."

"So, I take it you enjoy reading?" he asked.

"Oh yes! I love to read and have grown tired of rereading the few books Beatrice and I brought with us."

"You and your sister are welcome to borrow from my study. My only request is you return them to the approximate place you find them. I should have considered making the books available to you both earlier. My apologies," he offered.

"You probably did not call me here to discuss books," she said with a slight smirk.

Lucas arched a brow. She was audacious. His mother had her hands full, he thought, glancing to the right of his desk where a packet from Branson, his man of business, waited. It contained information for his consideration. There were candidates Branson had pre-screened for him that needed immediate attention. "I wanted to keep you from getting into trouble with the duchess. You may not realize it, but young ladies do not approach guests and ask to ride their horses. Although, I realize your enthusiasm has a habit of carrying you away." He watched her blush furiously at his remarks, gratified. She needed to get the point.

"Your Grace, I had not realized. I . . . guess I did, but I love horses, and you are right. I became carried away with the moment," she said, hanging her head slightly.

"I am not angry, Cat," he said, using the nickname she had offered. "I enjoy your spunk, although it needs tempering."

"You have my promise to do better," she offered contritely. Gone was the smirk.

"Good. We shall consider this behind us," Lucas said. "Now . . . have a good time."

"Meow!" grumbled Greyson.

Cat placed the kitten down, and the animal walked beside her down the hall. He marveled at the level of obedience she had coaxed from the kitten. Cats had always seemed too independent of rules, but the young girl had a way with animals. She is a lot like Harriett, he thought—so independent and a charmer. He wondered how Cat and her sister would relate to Harriett. *What was he thinking? Why did everything lead back to thoughts of Harriett?*

CHAPTER NINETEEN

T HE SISTERS ARRIVED in the front of the manor house in time to see their father swing onto the seat of his favorite chestnut.

"Father, where are you going?" Harriett asked, as she climbed from the coach. Her father ignored her question. She would not have asked, except his hair was unkempt, and his cravat was missing—an appearance totally unlike her father.

"I told you! He intercepted that message earlier," hissed Alice in her ear.

He glared at her and nudged his mount away, ready to leave.

"Wait, Father—please!" she cried after him, befogged by his hostility.

He stopped and turned the horse around, facing her. "Yes. Why would you have messages delivered here?" he growled.

"Uh. Because I live here—at least for a few more days. I had expected a message from my solicitor," she said calmly, hoping to pull something, anything, from her father that might tell her what was going on, or at least, if she received a message from Viscount Dudley.

"You got a message, all right, but not from your solicitor. You were not expecting anything else?" he asked, his tone cool.

"No. Just that one. My solicitor is working on something for me," she answered, realizing her responses were not forthcoming, but it *was* her business. "How strange. I wonder who else knew to reach me here." She held his gaze.

His scowl softened, but his voice remained gruff. "Perhaps I should be with you when you read it," he decided, signaling for the footman to take his horse. "Meet me in my study."

"What strange behavior for our father," Alice whispered under her breath. "Based on what I overheard earlier, he plans to question you about Lord Dudley—*the new one.*"

"Honestly, I have wracked my brains over what the viscount wants of me. Whilst I lived there, he barely said a word to me. Now, his persistent messages do nothing but irritate me. Perhaps he found out about the money," Harriett muttered.

"What money?" Alice pursued, still whispering.

Harriett whirled in her sister's direction. "Shh! I cannot say more now," she whispered through clenched teeth, handing Nichols her wrap and hat. As much as she adored her, sometimes Alice could be quite obtuse. "Can we discuss this later?"

"Certainly," her sister replied, hurt clear in her voice.

"Welcome, my ladies," Nichols said in his usual solemn tones. "A message was just delivered for you, Lady Harriett. The duke's man awaits a response." His lowered tone bespoke his understanding of what was taking place. The retainer had been loyal to her family for years, but always seemed to have a soft spot for her and her sister. He skillfully passed the message into Harriett's hand.

She quickly opened the note and gave it a quick glance before sliding it into her pocket. "Thank you, Nichols. Tell him yes," Harriett said in hushed tones before turning again to her sister.

"Who is the message from?" Alice asked.

"Really, Alice!" Harriett whispered angrily, taking a quick glance behind them before heading toward her father's study.

She would spend more time with Lucas' note later. She had no intention of letting her father know about it. "Right now, it is Father that I am concerned about. His attempts at intimidation have become intolerable," she continued to her sister, as Alice struggled to keep up.

The heavy door slammed shut as her father walked around Alice and followed Harriett into the room. Harriett noticed Alice had remained in the hall. She hated being harsh with her sister, painfully realizing it still annoyed her that Alice had always been Father's favorite and had had the type of marriage Harriett had hoped to have. She was not jealous, just angry. Angry at their parents for putting her on the proverbial block to pay off a debt— one that probably never should have been accrued.

"Why is Viscount Dudley . . . the new one," her father sneered, "Reaching out to you? What are the two of you *colluding* about?"

"*Collusion?* What are you speaking about, Father? I have no desire to have anything further to do with that family," Harriett returned, barely suppressing hysteria at the suggestion, while squeezing her fisted hands in the folds of her dress.

"You and the viscount are conspiring against me. How could you even consider becoming a part of his game?" he disparaged, his voice taunting.

"I know not what you speak of, Father," she said, drawing up her arms to her chest.

"You can drop the pretense. I wondered how you could afford to buy all these fancy clothes," Father said, waving a hand toward the day dress. "And you received a missive from the man a week ago."

"Do you have a letter intended for me, Father? First, I cannot imagine what you are talking about, and second, letters addressed to me are no concern of yours," she railed, her fury growing. She had forgotten that her father had been there when Mr. Jenkins had delivered the first message from Lord Dudley.

He reached into his pocket and withdrew the note, tossing it at her.

Harriett picked it up from the floor in front of her and read it. It was a note from Lord Dudley telling her he needed to see her. She planned to ignore this one, as she had done the first. She felt no obligation to see him. Something pricked at her neck. *Who had delivered it?* "Father—did Nichols say what the man looked like?"

"No. And I would find it extremely unusual, had Nichols done so," her father bit off, holding an opened missive toward her, showing the Dudley seal.

The door opened, and her mother stepped inside the room, remaining at the door. "Charles, please stop. She is your daughter. Enough."

Her father glared at her mother until she backed from the room wordlessly, which further infuriated Harriett. "You are wrong about this, Father. And you are wrong about me. If anyone has conspired, it was you. You used me to pay off some sort of debt you probably should never have incurred. You are a fool, Father," she said, snatching the opened note from her father's hand and storming from the study under a full head of steam. Her layered skirts swished around her legs as she hurried down the hall to the stairs. She raced up the stairs to her room.

Harriett grabbed the bedroom doorknob and slammed the door behind her with as much strength as she possessed, then leaned back against the heavy oak. With her heart pounding and feeling out of breath, she remained there, trying to regain her composure. The tears she had stubbornly held back ran unrepentant down her cheeks. *There is nothing left for me. Why am I still here?*

Her sister tapped on the door. "Harriett, it is me. Please let me in."

"Enter," she said, moving to her vanity mirror and checking the brimming tears.

Another tap sounded, followed by Jane, who entered carrying a pitcher of chocolate and biscuits.

"Thank you, Jane. We will pour it," Alice said, indicating the table between the fireside chairs.

"Yes, your ladyship," the maid said, giving a quick curtesy before leaving.

Alice turned to her sister. "We should talk."

"I have much to say, but I feel too angry at this moment," mumbled Harriett.

"You need to clear this up with Father," suggested Alice, "although, after today's display, I understand your reluctance."

"It is not reluctance. It is fury!" seethed Harriett. "I cannot understand anything having to do with Father."

"He has become very secretive," agreed Alice, "almost as if he is hiding something. But I cannot imagine what it could be. Mother seems just as vexed."

"I want to care, but Father has done his best to show his displeasure at my being here, and I can bear the hurt he has heaped upon me no longer," she said, swiping at a rogue tear.

"When you left, Father seemed to withdraw. It was as if he could not accept what had happened," Alice soothed. "As a grown woman, I see he has pushed Mama away, as well."

"Yes. I noticed," murmured Harriett. "Foolishly, I thought my family would welcome me home, not having seen everyone for the five years of marriage. I came home after mourning because I missed my family."

"This is about more than you, dear sister. I fear Father's wounds are just as deep, but for different reasons." Alice pulled her chair close and picked up her sister's hands, clasping them. "Why do you think Dudley is tracking you down? What does your gut tell you?"

Harriett shook her head slightly as she glanced away. "I am not sure. But I think it must have something to do with the money left in an account with my name on it." He wanted it back, and she had no intention of handing it over. Her solicitor had assured her it was hers, alone.

"That makes sense. What do you plan to do?" Alice asked.

"I plan to leave as soon as I can, once my solicitor finds me a new home," Harriett replied in a solemn tone.

"Until you sort everything regarding your new home, I insist you stay with me. I can return anytime. I came here to be with you." She squeezed Harriett's hands gently. "I missed you so much."

"That is very kind. However, my solicitor knows I plan to stay at the townhouse in Mayfair until I make other arrangements." She looked at her sister. "You may stay with me," she said with a tear-stained grin.

"What about the girls? The duchess is counting on our help," pressed Alice, taking her seat.

Harriett sat down and poured each of them some chocolate. "Perhaps this will help my mood," she said, passing a cup to her sister.

"It always helps mine!" laughed Alice. "You know what else helps my mood?" Her sister's grin broadened. "Shopping."

"I suppose we can do that," Harriett replied.

"Good!" Alice placed her cup on the table between the chairs. "I will leave you to rest." Her sister leaned down and kissed Harriett on the head. "Father will come around."

"I will see you in the morning." Harriett let out a breath and closed the door. She walked to her bed and kicked off her shoes, sat down, and leaned back. *Alice is right*, she thought. *There is the commitment I made to the duchess to help Lucas' girls.* A sigh escaped her as she closed her eyes. Thoughts of Lucas flooded her mind. Her lips tingled as she relived his kisses, wishing there had been more. She wanted him, but not just as a lover. *He made it clear he wants nothing to do with rekindling our relationship. Yet, I love him.*

Remembering the missive in her pocket, she withdrew it. Breaking the seal, she read:

Harriett,

Please allow me to see you tomorrow afternoon. I can come at three of the clock.

> *There are things I need to say.*

Fondly,
Lucas

Fondly? Dear God, he *has* relegated me to his past. A teardrop hit the page as she folded the paper and replaced it in her pocket. Fine, she would see him, but mostly out of courtesy. He had already said they had no future together. What more did he need to say that he had not already made clear?

First, she would keep her promise to Alice and go to town in the morning. They would return by noon, allowing her to see him in the afternoon. Harriett had no plans to cast her sister aside for a man she would never have.

INSTEAD OF INTERVIEWING candidates for a governess—something he *needed* to do—Lucas gazed out the window of his study, standing with his hands clasped behind him. However, his focus was not in front of him. He felt pulled and his soul ached. If he could avoid Harriett for a few more days, and if he never smelled another rose, he might find his way past what had become a physical ache emanating from his chest. Neither felt likely, he thought, realizing that his mother's rose garden spanned the entire back gardens. Pink and white roses were her favorite, although it was not his mother that wore the scent. *Harriett did.*

The ache had gotten worse since being locked in the orangery with her and he had acted as a cad, a rogue who thought all he needed to do was brush her lips with his and she would open herself for his physical attention. Yet, he understood the attraction was much more than physical. It was heartfelt, real, and he feared it would not leave when she did.

The door to his study opened and his friends entered behind him, each ignoring him and taking a seat in front of the fireplace on the wall to his left. He turned and smiled at the sound of the clinking of glasses. Clarendon had poured healthy measures of his favorite scotch. His drink waited on the side table near an empty chair that sat between them.

"Stop brooding and come sit with us," Clarendon said affably, giving a quick pat to the chair's cushion.

"I am not brooding. I am thinking," Lucas replied, taking the bait. "There is much to consider."

"You love her," Romney stated, candidly.

A thoughtful frown joined Lucas's brows. "I appreciate both of your concern, but it is not as simple as that. Harriett plans to leave as soon as her solicitor finds a suitable property, and she expects it could be any day, now."

"Unless you do something," prompted Clarendon. "It's none of my business, except you are my friend."

"I don't feel sure of anything. When I am around her, the old feelings flood through me, but they compete with the anger that helped heal my heart all those years ago," Lucas admitted. "I cannot set myself up for that kind of failure again."

"Who said it will end in failure this time?" Romney asked.

"You always had a knack for cutting through the noise and in a quiet voice, and making yourself heard, Romney," Lucas finally said, taking the proffered seat. Lucas picked up the glass and took a healthy swig.

"Thank God for that," Clarendon said, alluding to Romney's survival on the battlefield.

"Yes. I thank my lucky stars often," his friend responded. "But we are speaking of you, Dorman. Lady Dudley has not left Richmond yet. Do you not feel you owe it to you both to talk through what holds you back? It's obvious where your heart lies, even if not to you."

"Well said, Romney," Clarendon extolled.

"I will consider what you both have said," Lucas said before taking another long sip of his scotch. "Thank you for this." He saluted Clarendon with his glass. "I needed it."

"It's your whisky," his friend teased. "I merely poured it."

"What about a game of billiards? The women are taking tea somewhere today. We have most of the afternoon to do what we want to do before their return," Romney suggested.

"I rather like that idea. Two candidates for governess have

surfaced for interviews, but that need not happen today. Edgerton can arrange the interviews for later," Lucas said, grinning. "I thought to visit the stables and see how Colton is doing with the jockey. Afterwards, let's play billiards."

"That sounds like a good plan," Clarendon agreed.

Romney and Clarendon were both right. Lucas needed to speak to Harriett. He would do that tomorrow. He rang for the footman. "I will meet you both downstairs in ten minutes," he said, walking back to his desk.

The two men nodded and left the room, as Lucas withdrew a sheet of vellum from the drawer. Quickly, he composed a message to Harriett, asking her if he could call tomorrow afternoon.

A tap at the door sounded, and Trask opened the door and gave a bow. "How can I be of help, Your Grace?"

"Trask, deliver this to Lady Dudley at Canton Manor and await a response," Lucas said, affixing his wax seal. "And ask Mrs. Nettles to prepare a tray of food and drink to be brought to the billiard room in two hours."

"Yes, Your Grace," the footman said, bowing and exiting.

Tomorrow he would see Harriett. Today, he planned to have fun with his friends. Once he had settled this in his mind, a strange feeling of relief overcame Lucas. *My friends are right. I need to sort this out.*

CHAPTER TWENTY

The next day

HARRIETT AWOKE TO a chilly room. She glanced toward the fireplace and noticed the embers needed stoking. Unwilling to lie in bed any longer, she sat up and leaned against the pillows, watching her still sleeping puppy on the pillow next to hers. She watched while Penelope's paw jerked slightly, followed by whimpering noises. Grinning, she realized the puppy had to be dreaming. *She needs to get out and play,* she realized, dragging herself from her bed, determined to take Penelope for a walk. It looked chilly, with sparse, tufted clouds high in the clear, blue sky. She shivered slightly when she touched the cold window-pane, satisfied her pelisse and some warm gloves would serve her need. A small groan emanated from her bed, and she laughed to see her puppy still on her back, stretching her paws in the air and waking up. *Just like a person*, she thought. *How funny!*

"Penelope, you make me smile, and sometimes I need that smile."

Jane walked in carrying a small brown package. "Your lady-ship, I measured Penelope and made her a small wrapper. 'Tis not bitter cold, but the wee dog does not have the thick coat other dogs have."

"That's very considerate, Jane. Thank you very much for that kindness. It should be perfect for a day like today," Harriett said, fingering the soft woolen fabric. "It's an amazing duplicate of the blue one I plan to wear!" She turned to her puppy, who by now was standing on all fours and stretching out her front paws. "Jane, look at her. She acts like she hasn't a care in the world."

"True, yer ladyship. The pup does not seem to worry much," the maid said with a laugh.

"That looks like an amazing stretch, little one," Harriett said, feeling a twinge of envy for the pup's carefree attitude. It seemed like her worries had mushroomed to include her father's behavior, just when she thought to escape his nasty mood without incident. After living with Dudley, she had vowed to never allow a man to control her again. In that vein, she no longer recognized the man her father had become and wondered at the change. *My gut tells me it is Dudley and the deal he made to marry me to him, although I believed my marriage had satisfied the debt. Why does he still behave this way . . . unless there is something more.*

"Come here, Penelope. This will keep you warm," Harriett said, picking up her puppy and placing him in her lap to affix the garment. "I like the closure. You have even provided for her to grow a little! Thank you so much, Jane." Setting the dog down on the floor, they admired the coat together as Penelope strutted back and forth, as if she were modeling it.

Harriett secured the end of Penelope's leash around her wrist as they walked around the garden. Leaves suddenly rustled behind her and she spun around to see a man standing there. She jumped back, but Penelope jerked Harriett's arm when she ran forward, tugging against the lead, growling, and barking.

"Do not be alarmed, my lady," the man said, taking a step toward her. "I mean no ill will."

"Why are you hiding in our shrubbery?" she demanded, fisting her hands to control the fright, and ignoring her trembling shoulders.

"Sorry to scare you, my lady. Lord Dudley demanded that I find you and give you this, with the message that it is in your best interest to see him today," he replied.

Harriett reached down to quiet her dog and tried quelling the sudden nausea that threatened to cast up her accounts. "You . . . I recognize you. Mr. Jenkins. This sounds like a threat." At least her voice sounded strong.

"'Tis not a threat, my lady. He is most determined to meet with you," Jenkins said. "He is not like the former lord, your husband, but it would be advisable to meet with him," the man rejoined, "especially since he seems most determined to meet with you. I left a message for you yesterday but was not at all sure you would receive it, so I tried again today."

The missive Father had intercepted. "The viscount wants me to travel to Kent for a *meeting*. Ridiculous," she scoffed. "No." She finished with that family and planned to never cross paths with her shrew of a mother-in-law again. Despite her bravado, an involuntary shudder escaped.

"Lord Dudley is here. He asked me to emphasize the urgency of meeting with him," Jenkins continued.

Harriett started. "Where?" she squeaked the word in alarm. Penelope tugged against her tether, and alternately began to bark and growl furiously, pawing the ground to reach the man.

"'Tis quite the guard dog you have, your ladyship," he sniggered, his tone mocking.

"She's caused enough stir to draw attention," Harriett snapped.

"Here is your message. Lord Dudley said it is urgent you heed it," he said, shoving a note at her. "His lordship will find you; you will not need to seek him out." The man turned on his heel and walked away.

"Wait," Harriett said.

He stopped and allowed Harriett and Penelope to catch up with him.

"You mentioned earlier, he is not like my husband. What do you mean?" Harriett asked, unnerved by the knowledge Lord Dudley had followed her to Richmond, demanding to meet. If he demanded the money, her solicitor had already assured her he had no right to it. Surely, he realized that. Recalling her mother-in-law's chants, Harriett knew nothing would stop Lord Dudley from pursuing the money if he chose to. Still, if he wanted the money, would he not have just said so? *If not the money, what else could he want?*

Jenkins thought for a moment, and when he answered, his tone was softer. "He is not unkind, your ladyship. Meet with him." With that, he left.

Harriett stood there, staring at his back as he walked out of her view. She opened the missive and read it.

Lady Dudley,

I have just arrived in town and need to meet with you. There are important matters you need to know about. We must meet to discuss these issues. I will find you. This needs to be kept confidential.

Yours truly,
Viscount William H. Dudley

How odd! The message alluded to *matters*, with no mention of money. She had felt so certain it was her inheritance. She had known the Dudley family to be greedy scrappers, willing to do anything to get money. Surely, he would have mentioned the money if it had to do with it.

Moments later, she heard hooves and relaxed, realizing Jenkins had ridden away. She wondered how long he had been here, watching for her.

"Harriett, there you are!" her sister's higher pitched voice startled her from her momentary reverie.

Alice walked up and looked around. "I would have sworn I heard voices—yours and someone else's. Were you talking to someone?" she asked, continuing to glance about the grounds as she approached Harriett's side.

"No," Harriett answered quickly, deciding not to tell her

about Jenkins' visit. She realized she had just seen Lord Dudley. "I was talking to Penelope. I am afraid I was pretending to be Penelope and a red squirrel, and made up a deeper voice for the squirrel," she lied. "Penelope has been growling and barking at a squirrel, who obviously has thrown good sense to the wind to tease my dear puppy. I think her guttural growl must have frightened the dear thing away." She took her sister by the arm. "Walk with us. Penelope seems to enjoy her walk and I do not have the heart to drag her back inside just yet."

"Certainly," murmured Alice.

"Did you need me?" Harriett asked, mildly concerned about the pensive mood of her sister, and wondering if she had heard any part of the conversation. "I left word with Jane that I was taking Penelope for a walk." Alice was the type that would eventually talk about it. Best to wait her out.

"Yes, actually. I find I need to do some urgent shopping. I brought a new red pelisse for Christmastide and realized I forgot to pack the hat I had made for it. I wondered if you would enjoy accompanying me to town," her sister replied, still sounding a little distracted.

"I recall you showing me the red pelisse and loved the color red you chose."

"Yes, that's the one," Alice murmured, looking at her sister with an odd expression on her face.

"That sounds lovely!" replied Harriett. A trip to town could soothe her nerves. It was just the thing she needed. "I would love to order a new hat and perhaps we can find Penelope a new toy!"

"You made up a voice for the squirrel?" Alice asked, sounding bewildered.

"I did. Perhaps it will be my puppy voice. Penelope enjoyed the banter," she continued. She found talking like that with Penelope amusing and could see it continuing. It made her feel less alone. "Did you like that?" she asked her pup in as deep a voice as she could muster.

The dog's ears stood up, and she barked back.

"Perhaps that was what I heard," Alice admitted, more cheerfully. "Would you like a new toy, Penelope?" her sister said, in a childlike voice.

"See? It is fun to talk with her," Harriett inserted.

"Yes, it is!" returned Alice. "Or perhaps a new hat to go with Penelope's adorable wrap!" she said again in the childish voice.

"Oh! I love that idea," Harriett contended. "It can match mine." Crouching down to eye level with her puppy, she adopted her puppy voice. "Would you enjoy that, dearest Penelope?"

"Arf, arf," her puppy returned, causing both sisters to giggle.

THE DAY HAD gotten off to a sluggish, nay, painful start, as far as Lucas was concerned. He and his friends had played billiards until the wee hours of the morning. Played billiards and consumed brandy . . . at least in the beginning. He was not sure when it changed to scotch, but both his head and stomach hurt. He looked up at the ceiling, which appeared to move, and stuck his foot onto the floor, anchoring himself. Smiling at the minor success, he closed his eyes, hoping he could ease at least one of the remaining problems. Luckily, the only real meeting he had today was the one he had arranged with Harriett. Trask reported her answer was *yes*. One word. No note. *Had he hoped for more?* He had not given her anything more than *no*, along with conflicting behavior. As a result, she planned to leave and soon. However, his friends were right. It was now or never if he wanted to claim her for his own. Lucas realized he would wither inside if she married another.

The door to his room opened and Wilson entered, walking first to the deep green velour curtains, and swishing them open, and then to his bedside. Sunlight streamed onto the bed, appearing to ricochet off the white linens.

Lucas groaned, and threw his pillow over his head, hoping to block out Wilson and the light. "What the hell, Wilson?"

"You gave me orders that I wake you, Your Grace," the man said, his tone even. "I fetched one of Mrs. Nettles' cures." He placed the drink on the table next to Lucas' bed. "The sooner you drink it, the sooner you will feel more like yourself."

"Tell me the others have also requested something similar," Lucas muttered. "They matched me drink for drink."

Wilson remained quiet.

"What? Am I the only one foxed this morning?" he demanded.

"Begging your pardon, Your Grace, but your friends are downstairs with their wives breaking their fast," the valet replied.

"Damn and blast it! Some host I am," Lucas said, dragging both legs to the side of the bed and picking up the glass of Mrs. Nettles' potion.

"Hold your nose. If you do not, that will create an entirely different problem," Wilson warned. "I had to hold it away, myself."

Lucas laughed. "If this does not work, it may not matter." He held his nose and drank the concoction down, twisting his face in distaste.

"Good!" exhaled Wilson. "Mr. Branson is waiting in your study."

"I had not expected him this morning. Ring for Trask and have him invite Branson to join us in the breakfast room and break his fast. If he refuses, let him know I plan to do so before meeting with him." Although Lucas only planned to get tea and a biscuit. The mere thought of food added to his discomfort. "I should not be long."

"Very good, Your Grace. "Your shave and bath are ready."

"Thank you, Wilson."

A half-hour later, Lucas joined his friends in the breakfast room. Romney and Clarendon were reading the paper and their wives were sitting with his mother, chatting. "Good morning!" he said, entering the room.

Clarendon gave a sly look over the top of the paper. "How are you feeling?"

"Good. Why do you ask?" Lucas replied innocently, causing both men to snicker.

"What?" he bantered, good-naturedly.

"We are surprised to see you, is all," Romney said.

"I confess, my head felt like it had been through a log-splitter," Lucas conceded.

"I notice you are not eating," Romney said, wearing a grin.

"All right. I guess I was feeling sorry for myself," said Lucas. "I will take your advice."

"What advice is that, my darling son?" inquired his mother from the other end of the table.

He debated answering her, but she would just bait him until he told her. "I plan to visit Lady Dudley and discuss a few things—later today."

"Ah. She is a darling girl. It is about time you came to your senses," she challenged, sipping her tea.

He glanced about at the smiles on the faces of everyone in the room. "You assume it will be more than a conversation?"

"I do not think we are assuming, son. Rather, we are hoping," his mother quipped.

He could not pretend he did not have feelings for Harriett. "Mother, it remains to be seen if your hard work to bring us together will have the ending you seek," he said with a wink.

All three men chuckled as his mother gave a practiced look of feigned shock. He looked about and realized the girls were missing. "Where are Beatrice and Cat?"

"I expect Beatrice and Catherine at any minute," his mother replied, emphasizing her disapproval of the nickname. "Catherine has requested to meet with you. She seems upset about some-thing and would not speak with me about it."

Had he been too harsh with the girl? "I wonder what that could be about. Let her know I have a short meeting with Mr. Branson and can meet with her when he leaves. He showed up without an appointment, so it must be important." Lucas had felt much more himself and decided to test his stomach. He motioned for Trask. "A light serving of potatoes and rashers," he said.

"Yes, Your Grace," the footman said, moving to carry out his request.

"Will you join us for a ride?" Romney asked.

"Perhaps a short one, after I meet with . . . Catherine," he said, in deference to his mother.

A short time later, he walked to his study to meet with Mr. Branson. "I am sorry to keep you waiting, Branson. We had hoped you would join us."

"I appreciated the invitation, Your Grace. However, I fear I overindulged when I broke my fast this morning," his man of business said, gently tapping his belly. "I had some news that I thought you could find of interest, and of course, we have the matter of the governess," he offered, pulling some vellum from his leather satchel.

"I see," Lucas said, nodding.

"One of the young women whose information I presented has accepted another position and has advised me she no longer wishes to be considered. The other one plans to marry, so I brought you two more suitable candidates. These ladies are a little older and may be better contenders." Branson leaned back in his chair while Lucas regarded the dossier. "I gained some information you may be interested in, in passing, of course. However, since there was a previous relationship, I thought you should be aware."

"The lady?" Lucas questioned. "What lady and what information?" He no longer cared if his tone had an edge to it. Did everyone know about his interest in Lady Dudley?

"Well, let me make sure I get this straight," Branson said, startled at Lucas' tone. "You probably know we have seen Lady Harriett Dudley in town. Her family are your neighbors, after all."

"Go on." Lucas bit his tongue to keep from saying more. He

may look for a new man of business before the afternoon ended.

"It appears the new Viscount Dudley—her husband's heir—has been searching for Lady Harriett Dudley—first in London, and now, here in Richmond."

"Why? Is he here now?" Lucas asked in disbelief.

"I cannot be certain, but I believe he may be," Branson said.

"I wonder if Harriett is aware . . ." Lucas mused aloud.

"I do not believe so, Your Grace, but it is my assumption. There is also a rather large man . . . a Mr. Jenkins . . . that has made inquiries on the viscount's behalf in both London and here on her whereabouts. I found out about it by accident in a tavern."

"Her ladyship does not frequent taverns," Lucas snapped.

"Yes. But people that work in the places she frequents do, Your Grace," Branson stated.

"So, there are possibly two of them. How unusual the viscount would follow her to Richmond where her family lives. What could he want with her?" Lucas deliberated.

"As I heard it, her late husband's mother has been rather vocal, alleging Lady Dudley stole their money. However, word is her late husband bequeathed her money. The old woman vows to anyone listening they will have it back. Perhaps that is what he is here to collect," Branson said, removing a pair of gold-rimmed spectacles from his inner pocket and adjusting them on his nose.

"Good to know, Branson. Thank you. I am glad you shared that. I may . . . uh . . . run into Lady Dudley and would want to know these things in case they called upon me to assist her with matters." Lucas felt too antsy to sit. This whole thing disturbed him. There was no doubt the viscount would find Harriett. He wanted this meeting over so he could reach her, although if he were to arrive too early at her home, things may not go as he hoped. "Thank you for bringing this to my attention, Branson."

"There are a few other items I need your signature on," Branson said, standing.

"Thank you. Leave them on the corner of my desk and I shall get them back to you once I have time to read them." He had learned long ago not to sign anything without reading it—not that he distrusted Branson. But he had no wish for Branson or anyone to take advantage.

"Are we done?" he asked, walking to the door.

"Yes, Your Grace," Branson said, walking out and meeting Trask, who was passing in the hall. "I will let you know if I hear anything else."

"Thank you. Trask will walk you out."

Lucas sat behind his desk, perplexed over the next steps. Should he warn Harriett? Her father wanted nothing to do with him—not that he cared. That ship had sailed long ago. The man had sold his daughter into a despicable circumstance, and he no longer cared one way or the other for him. Before he could leave the room, the door opened, and Cat walked into the room, hanging her head.

"If you have time, I would like to speak with you, Your Grace," his young ward said.

Determined not to show irritation, Lucas resisted a sigh. "Take a seat, Cat."

"Yes, Your Grace," Cat said, taking the seat Branson had just vacated.

He waited, giving her time to say what she needed to tell him. Finally, she spoke. "My sister is afraid you will send us away when you find out what I did." Her voice held a tremor.

"I would prefer to hear you out, but I have no plans to abandon my duty to you and your sister," he inserted abruptly. *What had she done this time?*

She looked him straight in the eyes. "It was my fault you and Lady Dudley got locked in the orangery. Greyson got loose, and I thought he ran into the opened door of the greenhouse. When I peered inside, I saw you with Lady Dudley. Greyson meowed behind me, and I closed the door without realizing it had locked. After seeing you inside, I became frightened, scooped up Greyson, and ran into the house. I apologize, Your Grace."

"How did it lock?" he asked in a dry tone.

She gave a blank look. "I . . . am not sure." She paused. "Do . . . do you like Lady Dudley?"

The girl was impertinent, but hard not to like. Lucas fought the impulse to tell her it was not her business. Instead, he said, "I do."

Cat smiled broadly.

He had no reason not to believe her. It was an innocent mistake. Well, not innocent. But a mistake. It seemed Lady Catherine had a penchant for making them. She kept things interesting, to be sure. "Did you hear me calling?"

She shook her head.

"Is there anything else you would like to tell me?" he asked, gentling his voice.

"Only one. Beatrice told me to keep my mouth closed about it, but if you please, Your Grace, I would rather have a mother than a governess," she said, swiping at the corner of an eye.

"I am not sure I can deliver that, Cat. Even if I could, you still need a governess. I want the very best for you and your sister— educationally as well as socially," he explained. "This situation may never have occurred, had there been a governess." Lucas wondered how much she had seen with Harriett but decided not to ask.

"Is that all you needed to tell me?"

She nodded. "Thank you, Your Grace," she said, getting up and curtseying. "I will leave you to your business."

"Cat, thank you for being honest and coming to me." He realized he never would have known how he became locked in the greenhouse otherwise.

"You're welcome," his ward said with a smile, before leaving the room and closing the door behind her.

He had promised to ride with his friends, but he felt sure they would understand his absence. Lucas could not explain it, but he had an intense need to see Harriett.

CHAPTER TWENTY-ONE

"LADIES! 'TIS A pleasure to see you both again. What can I do for you?" Mrs. Toppin asked, as Alice and Harriett entered the milliner's shop.

"Harriett and I need a couple more new hats for our new pelisses. Mine is red, so I need something to match," Alice said cheerfully.

"Yes, and I would like to have one to match this blue one, and a small one that I can tie on my little dog," Harriett added, grinning.

"That is a most unusual order, but I believe it is very doable," the older woman returned with a glimmer of laughter in her eyes. "I have never made a hat for a dog, but it is a project I welcome."

"She is a most unusual dog. My abigail made her a small wrap to match my blue pelisse and it would be adorable to have a small hat that resembled my own. I do not expect it to be very large."

"Yes, my lady. I can envision one. I do not suppose you have the measurements of her head. However, if you can show me with your hand, I can get a good idea. We can adjust it," the milliner said.

Harriett put her hands together and fashioned what she thought resembled the size of Penelope's head. Alice nodded her approval.

"Perfect," Mrs. Toppin cheered, measuring the space. "I will make it tie. The fabric should allow for adjustment."

"Lovely!" Harriett exclaimed. "Alice, would you mind if I ran next door and spoke with Mrs. Thimblesby? While she is working on my order, I thought about adding a couple of things before we go to the bookstore."

"Certainly. I will not be but twenty minutes," her sister said, giving a slight nod in the seamstress's direction.

"Thank you. I will meet you there," Harriett said, walking out the door.

As she walked toward the shop, a black-lacquered carriage slowed just ahead of her, and the door opened. The door had the familiar gold, scrolled D.

"Lady Dudley. Can I have a word with you? It is very important." She recognized the voice of the new viscount. He had found her. Stopping, she glanced inside. There was only him, although she recognized Mr. Jenkins sitting in the seat next to the driver. She started to refuse, but hesitated.

"I only want to drive a few blocks so I can share some important information and I shall return you. It is most important—more so than you can imagine. On my word, I will return you to this spot as soon as I give you this information," Lord Dudley urged.

"You make it sound mysterious," she said, as she nibbled her lip and looked about. It would most likely be a half-hour before Alice left the milliner's shop, she reasoned. Her sister loved hats. The heir, as she referred to him, had never been unkind to her. Although, he was rarely in her company the entire year of mourning. Deciding to hear him out, she stepped up to the carriage door. "My sister will worry about me if I am not in the modiste's shop when she looks for me. Give me ten minutes in case she is with a customer."

"Yes. I can do that. This will not take long," Lord Dudley said.

Harriett went into the seamstress's shop, ordered her shifts, and asked Mrs. Thimblesby to let Alice know she would return shortly. The shop owner assured she would. As Harriett left the shop, she noticed the woman watching her from behind the curtain as she entered the carriage. He shut the door behind her, and the carriage lurched forward. "Can we make this quick, Lord Dudley?"

He gave an odd look of relief on his face. "I have looked for you, because I found some papers that I did not want to fall into anyone else's hands," he said, adding to the mystery. "However, understanding your relationship with my cousin, I felt you should have the papers."

"You have my attention," she said, sitting across from him. So far, he had made no mention of money. Interesting.

"I found some purposely hidden papers while working in my office. They forced you to marry the former viscount."

She nodded. "Yes."

"Because it appears your husband blackmailed your father," the viscount stated.

"How? Why?" she asked, forgetting all the apprehension she had felt before.

"The crux of it is your father had a habit of visiting a certain tavern in London. On a particular night, he became very foxed and when he awoke, they had covered him with blood and made him believe he had killed someone. Lord Dudley . . . *your husband* . . . promised your father he had taken care of it. But what began was a long process of blackmail levied against the earl. Unfortunately, it was not the only evidence of blackmail I found. Dudley apparently found it lucrative. He collected sworn statements, signed by witnesses—which I find highly suspicious. I also found a paper detailing a death that took place at about the same time in that same tavern, which resulted in an arrest. He blackmailed your father and leveraged a death your father had nothing to do with."

The viscount passed papers to Harriett. "Your husband had another accomplice—a baron—but I cannot determine his name. Since your husband died, they cannot hold him accountable, and without knowing the other name, it would be hard to pursue. But should these papers fall into the hands of someone who stands to gain from such a venture, your father could still be vulnerable."

Harriett could not believe what she was hearing. It explained a lot. "You mean his mother," she murmured.

"I cannot say," he returned. "However, these papers are yours. You can try to pursue the incident. Or let it go. As near as I can determine, your father probably left town without knowing they arrested someone else. Lord Dudley—your husband—used your father's drunken state to make a tidy sum of money and apparently, gain a wife."

"I cannot believe . . . thank . . . thank you," Harriett stammered.

"Lady Dudley, the treatment you endured . . . my housekeeper showed me the windows to your rooms that were nailed shut, and I have heard so much more. I am ashamed of what happened to you and your family at the hands of my predecessor. Possibly, your father could have pursued this, but they stacked the deck against him. There may have been other circumstances these papers do not adequately provide. My advice to you is to destroy them," he said.

He spent some time going over the meaning of the papers he had given her. "These would have been damning evidence against your husband had they been discovered while he lived. But that would have been doubtful," he said with a grimace.

"You are very kind to do this." She did not know what to do but thank him. As they pulled back in front of the seamstress's shop, she noticed her family carriage had departed from across the street. "Something must have gone wrong. I left word you were taking me in your carriage for a brief ride. The modiste had promised to tell my sister."

"Perhaps we should find out what happened," he offered.

Numbly, Harriett tucked the papers back in the thin brown leather pouch he gave her and rolled it, placing it in an inside pocket the modiste had made in her pelisse. It was for the newspaper or a book but was perfect for the small packet of papers. He held open the door and helped her from the carriage.

"'Thank you' seems too little for what you have given me," she said, quietly.

"Nonsense. You were a victim of your husband's greed. It should have never happened. Let us try to find your sister before she thinks we have kidnapped you," he said, and they both laughed.

They tried the modiste's shop, first, but Mrs. Toppin told her she had not seen her sister in almost an hour. Realizing how much longer it had taken drove a sickening feeling to the pit of Harriett's stomach. What must Alice have thought? After the display with Father yesterday, this was the last thing she needed to happen.

The door to the modiste's shop jingled behind them as they entered. "Mrs. Thimblesby is Alice . . . Lady Penfield here?" Harriett asked.

"No, my lady. I am truly sorry. I saw her come in and look about for you, but I became busy with a difficult customer and could not leave to deliver your message. My sincere apologies. I hope everything is all right."

No, she feared everything was *not* all right. The store owner looked at Lord Dudley, waiting for an introduction, but Harriett was in no mood. "Thank you, Mrs. Thimblesby." She took Lord Dudley's proffered arm and exited the store.

"I can drive you home. The only urgency I felt was giving you the information. You can deal with it as you see fit," he offered. "I apologize for being so mysterious, but your father was blocking my every effort to see you."

"Yes. He has been difficult." Harriett stood there and laughed from relief, placing one of her gloved hands at her temple. "Lord Dudley, you do not know what I thought. Your messages fed my imagination. They told me little, and I feared the worst."

"The worst being?" he asked.

"You would return me to that house of horrors," she blurted, before covering her mouth in shock over having said it.

"You have nothing to feel bad about. I feel the same way. I replaced all the staff, except those that came with me and a select few in the stables. And, of course, the cook, who stayed far too busy to take part in the shenanigans. Your former mother-in-law has been moved to the dowager house, and is no longer welcome in the main house, nor any other properties. She raged about it, but it does her no good." he stated. "You may visit . . . if you ever have a need."

"There are too many memories . . . and none of them good," she said sadly. "For five years, he refused to allow me to wear what he did not purchase himself, see anyone when he was not by my side, he kept me confined to my room, and refused my requests to see my family. No one would help me. This seems like . . ."

"*Karma* is what the cook calls it," he inserted, laughing. "I like the woman. And she is an excellent cook."

"True! The woman brought me food up the servants' stairs when Dudley punished me, which was often," Harriett returned. "She was my only ally."

"My father will be so relieved when these are burned," she said. "I will allow him to do that once he explains it to my mother. Perhaps that can help heal the wounds my marriage caused everyone."

"Your sister and your family carriage are gone, I notice. Perhaps it would be better if I took you home. I will do my best to soothe any ruffled feathers I may have inadvertently created," the viscount offered.

"Yes! That would be better than sitting here."

He took his cane and tapped the ceiling of the coach, causing the carriage to lurch forward. "Take us to Canton Manor," he said from the window.

A few minutes later, two horses and their riders noisily overtook the carriage and demanded it to stop.

"Are we being set upon by highwaymen?" she asked shakily.

"I do not think so. Their faces are not covered. Unless I miss my guess, one of them is your father," Lord Dudley replied.

"STOP THE CARRIAGE!" Lucas called out. The carriage pulled off the road and stopped. Both men put their hands in the air. "I am not here to rob you. I am here to collect Lady Harriett Dudley. You have no right to take her."

The door opened, and Harriett stepped out, followed by a man he recognized as the new viscount. "Lucas ... *Your Grace* ... what are you doing?"

"Rescuing you, Harriett. Walk toward me," he directed. "You are Lord Dudley, correct?"

The man nodded.

"Then, please step back and allow her past," Lucas commanded.

"You came to save me?" Harriett echoed in disbelief, doing as he said.

"Yes," Lucas said, pulling her close. He tightened his arm around her, and heat shot up his arm and through this middle. This was more than just wanting her. He *needed* her to be his.

"Harriett, are you all right?" Lord Scarsdale walked from behind the coach, where he had left his horse. "Sir, you will leave my daughter alone. I may not have done right by her before, but I will never let her suffer pain, which should rightfully be mine alone to bear again."

"Father?"

Her father stepped between Harriett and the viscount, who Lucas noted wore a curious grin on his face.

"You do not understand, Father. Viscount Dudley has come to help you," Harriett pleaded.

"What do you mean, help me? This family has taken too much from me. I have even lost my pride to them, but no more. I will not lose my daughter twice," Scarsdale said emphatically.

"Sir, if you will allow your daughter to explain, the reason for my visit will become clear in minutes. I seek no harm for you or your family," Dudley explained. "Lady Dudley, would you like me to explain?"

Harriett nodded and allowed Lord Dudley to explain. She pulled out the papers and handed them to her father, who appeared numb.

"You would do this for me?" the earl said in a puzzled tone.

"It is the right thing to do," answered Lord Dudley. "Your daughter lived a tough existence at the hands of the previous viscount and his mother. Once I realized what she went through, I fired the staff and rehired new. When I found the papers, things became clearer to me, and I determined to find her and relieve her of the worries she left Kent with."

"Thank you," the earl said, unabashedly swiping at tears. "I am sorry to have not challenged this when it occurred." He turned to Lucas. "Forgive me, Your Grace, for what I did to you and to my daughter. I will never forgive myself."

Lucas opened his mouth, but closed it, knowing not what to say at this twist of events. Instead, he gave a curt nod.

Dudley turned to Harriett. "You have not mentioned the money you inherited from your husband. Your former mother-in-law has apparently tried many things to gain access, despite my warning her away. The money is yours. I have no legal claims to it. She has no claims, either."

"Thank you," she mouthed.

"My predecessor intended it to be a hidden account to use at his discretion," he explained. "However, he met his death, and you are the benefactor. When I found the papers detailing the subterfuge and the blackmail, I could have destroyed them, but then, you would not have known for sure you were safe. I wanted that for you . . . for your family."

This was not what Lucas had envisioned. He glanced from one to another as the viscount explained how he found the papers, as well as others that he has destroyed. "It is nothing as I imagined, Lord Dudley," Lucas expressed.

The viscount smiled. "Indeed! I am glad about that."

Words stuck in Lucas' throat. The day's ordeal had become an incredible convergence of facts and supposition that yielded a completely different outcome than anything he had expected. Had he not been a part of it, he would have laughed. Instead, all he felt was the emptiness that threatened his soul when her sister had run into her father's home screaming Harriett had been abducted. When she described the black carriage, he left. He could not lose her twice. Her father had followed, vowing to save his daughter from a crime he should have paid for himself. They charged toward town, hoping to find her.

Unwilling to let this day end without saying his piece, Lucas took Harriett's right hand and dropped to one knee. "I may find this entire episode hilarious one day . . . as long as I can be serious now for one moment."

"What are you doing, Lucas?"

"Harriett, you have never been one to overstate the obvious," he chuckled. "I realized before today that I could not lose you a second time. When Alice returned to your home without you, I nearly lost my mind thinking I had lost my chance with you."

"You were supposed to visit much later . . ." she started.

"My love," he cut in, kissing her hand. "Allow me to finish."

She smiled down at him and nodded.

"I love you, Lady Harriett Dudley. And I wish with all my heart to make you my wife . . . my duchess. Love for you fills me. It is more than wanting you . . . it is needing to make you mine. You are and have always been my true love. Will you agree to be my wife?" He extracted a small velvet bag from his waistcoat pocket and opened it, revealing a small gold band decorated in sapphires and diamonds.

"Yes! I will marry you, Lucas," she said, pulling him up.

His lips found hers, and hungrily, he kissed her deeply, without caring who witnessed their love. Pulling back, he whispered,

"I can get a special license and marry you, if you wish it."

"I do," she murmured for his ears alone.

"Ahem," her father said, clearing his throat. "If Lord Dudley is in accordance, perhaps he can ride your horse back to the house, and you two can finish your . . . discussion in the carriage," he said with twinkling eyes.

"I rather like that idea," Lord Dudley concurred. "I have ridden in that carriage too long and miss the feel of a horse."

Lucas allowed Dudley to ride Dirk, warmly touching the horse on the neck to reassure him. He then ushered Harriett into the carriage, eager to have her back in his arms. As the coach took off, he pulled her close and kissed her with a hunger he realized could not satisfy with a kiss. "Harriett," he breathed, kissing her ears, down her throat and across her decolletage. His hand felt beneath her skirts and eased up her calf, slowly feeling its way to its apex. At his touch, she gasped.

"Should I move my hand away?" he asked, while tenderly rubbing her inner thigh.

"No . . . I mean . . . perhaps. We are close to my father's home," she said as she shuttered her eyes. "My body and heart want you to continue . . ." she said, pushing back and sitting. "But I think we should wait."

His hands lingered a moment more, savoring the feel of her silky skin. "I have waited this long. I can wait a little longer," he said, deliberately taking his time removing his hand. At her feet, he slid off her shoe and kneaded her foot.

"Mmm . . . I do not think my feet have ever had a gentle-man's touch," she said.

"There will be no part of your body that can make that claim when I make love to you, my love," he breathed in her ear.

"Only if you allow me the same pleasure with your body," she said in a whisper.

Her words made him thrum with desire, and he brought his lips to her naked foot, blowing heat on her inner arch, causing her to tremble.

"I love you, Lucas," she panted, pulling his face to hers. "I have never stopped loving you."

"And I you," he replied. "I tried my best to ignore you, to bury you beneath the same anger that got me through the pain before. But it would not work. I came early to ask your father for your hand . . ."

"You did not have to do that," she said, interrupting him.

"But I did," he contradicted. "I wanted him to look me in the eye and tell me I had his blessing this time. When he did that, I saw pain in his eyes."

"I suppose I understand what he must have been going through. But I have lost so much time with you. Lucas, you are everything I wished for, and all I have dreamed of these five years," she said, kissing his face and curling her fingers around his.

"And I will make it my mission to ensure you never again mourn the loss of those five years," he said, closing his eyes and kissing her.

EPILOGUE

Late April 1818

"WHY MUST WE leave the bed, Lucas, darling? It is still early," Harriett cajoled. "Come back to bed. It is rare we get to languish in bed, and I want to enjoy it." She needed to give more time for everyone to get to the dining room and could think of no better way than making love to her husband.

"I suppose I am still flying high over Colton's run this week in Epsom," Lucas teased, leaning down, and picking up a feather from the bedside table and gently running it across her face and down her arm. "The odds were against him, but I knew our boy could pull it off!"

"And they were but practice runs. Think of how well he will do in the actual race!" It had thrilled everyone to see Colton's timed runs. Winning a race would be a vindication of sorts since the Prince Regent himself had not believed in the grey colt's worth. Watching the horse make it through his paces yesterday had thrilled her.

"The Regent has taken an interest in your grey, I understand. That is quite an accomplishment after the months of training," reminded his wife. "I think you have earned some extra time in bed."

"And what do we tell our friends and your sister and her

husband? We should not want to be the last ones to the table. They have arrived for our new gathering and will look forward to the activities you have planned, my love."

"I appreciate your including my sister. I have missed her so much these past five years, and she helped to bring us together."

"If you mean she was in cahoots with my mother, I suppose I must thank her for her help. Although it will only encourage the two of them. Yet . . . they saw something I was unwilling to see," he admitted.

"Come here, Your Grace." Harriett crooked her finger and patted the pillow next to her. "You started something with that feather, my dear, and no longer can leave this bed until you finish what you started," she said in a lusty voice. "You have stirred desires that are not met watching a horse race, however enticingly you describe it, unless, of course, you might be interested in doing both."

"I see," he said, rolling himself back into the bed and pulling her under him. "I suppose you desire a repeat of last night," he said, leaning down and kissing her neck.

"I do, my love," she said, trailing her finger down his chest. "But we do not have time for a total repeat . . ."

Lucas caught her mouth in a deep kiss, trailing kisses down to her center. "I plan to pleasure you before I lose myself in the abyss of pleasure," he said. "We will make time."

He positioned himself over her, familiar with her desires and needs, and probed her moist core until her body convulsed with need. "I love you, Harriett," he said, losing himself to their lovemaking.

An hour later, the newly minted Duke and Duchess of Dorman met their friends in the dining room, ready to break their fast.

"It was kind of you to host us," Harriett said, taking her seat next to their hostess. "The duchess may join us later. She has invested herself in getting Lady Beatrice ready for the Season, and breaking in the governess," Harriett said, grinning.

"Dorman is lucky to have you, Your Grace. With two wards—one that will come out later this Season—the household must be a busy one," Lady Romney said, sipping her tea. "It thrilled us to see you marry."

"Thank you, Lady Romney. It excites me to see Lucas surrounded by his friends. He missed them over the years when everyone went in different directions," Harriett said.

"Yes, and it gives the women a chance to know each other," Lady Romney added, sweetening her tea.

"Your Graces, I trust you slept well?" Lady Clarendon asked.

"We did," Harriett said with a wink, meant only for her friend.

Lady Clarendon smiled and passed the tray of Chelsea buns. "I understand these are a favorite. Your cook agreed to bake them for me. I hope you do not mind."

"Not at all!" Harriett took one of the Chelsea buns and accepted a cup of chocolate. "You have all my favorites."

"We try," Lord Clarendon said, taking a Chelsea bun for himself as they passed them around the table.

"Greetings, my friends," Lord Romney said as he entered the room. "What have I missed?"

A swish of satin skirts announced the entrance of Lady Alice Penfield and her husband, the Earl of Penfield. "Have I missed anything?" Her sister intoned, ignoring Harriett's stare. Alice had absolutely zero ability to keep a secret.

"You've almost missed the Chelsea buns, but nothing else . . . yet," Christopher Anglesey, the Marquess of Banbury, said, taking a bite from his bun. "Tell us about your horse, Dorman. I understand your stablehand's son, Frank, jockeyed him for you."

"Thank goodness for Lord Banbury," murmured Lady Penfield.

"Yes. The young man is ideal! He is small of stature, but big of heart, knows horses, and works Colton as much as he can without pushing him overly much. I would have never imagined finding a jockey with his skills," Lucas continued the conversation about his favorite diversion, rubbing his hands excitedly. "It still seems surreal that he may win with his progress."

"Is that not why you bought him?" Banbury observed.

"It was so exciting!" Lady Banbury exclaimed. "I had never seen a horse race, and vow not to miss any of your grey's future meets!"

"You are to take it easy, darling. You know what Dr. Fellows told you." Banbury looked at his friends. "Diana is due in a few months. The doctor gave her permission to come but cautioned her she must take it easy. He thinks we are having twins."

"Congratulations!" Harriett bade, quietly touching her own stomach. "That is wonderful news. Perhaps you will have a boy and a girl."

"Whatever it turns out to be, we will be elated," effused Banbury. "It was unexpected but welcomed news."

A tap sounded at the door and Egerton entered. "Your Grace, this arrived for you. I thought you should see it," the older retainer said, holding out the salver with a scrolled message on it.

Lucas took the scrolled message and unwrapped it, skimming it. He looked up at his friends. "The prince plans to visit the Epsom Derby in June for the race, but before it, requests an opportunity to watch Colton in some practice runs."

"Probably plans to bet on the horse!" Clarendon said excitedly. "He will attract attention and may boost your earnings."

"It is not so much about that. I believe in this horse and have since I first heard of his potential sale," Lucas protested.

"Does it not seem unusual that he is taking so much of an interest?" Harriett questioned, taking the note when he handed it to her. "However, I have never met the Prince Regent."

"You will do so soon," Clarendon said dryly, buttering his biscuit.

"The prince may try to take your grey back," teased Romney.

"That will not happen," laughed Dorman. "Colton has a home for himself at Pembley Manor. I have always wanted a good racehorse—since childhood!"

"Banbury, you could not be here when Sable arrived, but I have never been so surprised. Thank you sincerely. I am most appreciative of your help in securing her for me," Romney said, patting his friend on the back.

"We wanted to do that for you, Romney. Is she well? I understood her to be maintained very well," Banbury said. "Do you have her with you?"

"Of course! Perhaps we can ride later. I missed her and time spent with her seems a gift."

Harriett surveyed the room, realizing the richness of her life today. She had lost hope that she would ever be happy and doubted she would ever marry the man that held her heart. It had all happened to her. It was now or never. She started to rise but caught a look on Romney's face that seemed to ask her to wait. She nodded. Instead, he stood.

"As we are all gathered here, I thought it would be a good idea to remind Dorman of the bet in the betting book. Recall it?" Romney stood there grinning. He glanced at Harriett, who gave him a slight nod.

"I do," Lucas said, his eyes narrowing slightly. "Although whoever it was is a true foreseer of futures. I am extremely happy and for once, understand the delirium marriage offers." He coughed. "So, who was it?"

Romney looked around. "It was me," he said, beaming.

"Romney, of course it was you," the duke said.

Harriett stood and walked to her husband. Taking his hand, she looked into his eyes. "My dearest husband, in the autumn of this year, your new moniker will be 'Father.' Between now and then, we will need to think of a name for our precious boy or girl."

Lucas stared at her, tears brimming in his eyes. "I cannot think of anything I would like to do more, my dearest wife, than name this beautiful child." He glanced around the room and saw he was not the only one swiping at tears. "You kept this a secret . . ."

"Until I could be sure," she quickly added. "I thought you might enjoy sharing it with your closest of friends and family. We should share it with the girls. They will be thrilled, although I believe Bea may already be suspicious."

"We can speak with them about the adoption process we have initiated, as well. Perhaps it will feel much more like a family for them, and Cat will no longer worry about being sent to the orphanage," Lucas said with a laugh.

Harriett tittered. "Three months ago, I would have never wagered anything like this could happen for me, but nothing could make me happier. I feel as if I am living a dream!"

Romney raised a glass. "To our beloved friend, the Duke of Disorder. May your life and that of your lovely bride be forever full to the brim with the happiness and chaos that children add."

"Hear, hear," his friends and family sounded, with clinks of glasses.

"You will never have to bet on my love, Harriett," Lucas said, placing a finger beneath her chin and tipping her face to meet his. "Your love is the very nourishment of my soul. I look forward to all of our years together."

About the Author

Anna St. Claire is a big believer that *nothing* is impossible if you believe in yourself. She sprinkles her stories with laughter, romance, mystery and lots of possibilities, adhering to the belief that goodness and love will win the day.

Anna is both an avid reader author of American and British historical romance. She and her husband live in Charlotte, North Carolina with their two dogs and often, their two beautiful granddaughters, who live nearby. *Daughter, sister, wife, mother, and Mimi*—all life roles that Anna St. Claire relishes and feels blessed to still enjoy. And she loves her pets – dogs and cats alike, and often inserts them into her books as secondary characters. And she loves chocolate and popcorn, a definite nod to her need for sweet followed by salty...*but not together*—a tasty weakness!

Anna relocated from New York to the Carolinas as a child. Her mother, a retired English and History teacher, always encouraged Anna's interest in writing, after discovering short stories she would write in her spare time.

As a child, she loved mysteries and checked out every *Encyclopedia Brown* story that came into the school library. Before too long, her fascination with history and reading led her to her first historical romance—Margaret Mitchell's *Gone With The Wind*, now a treasured, but weathered book from being read multiple times. The day she discovered Kathleen Woodiwiss,' books, *Shanna* and *Ashes In The Wind*, Anna became hooked. She read every historical romance that came her way and dreams of writing her own historical romances took seed.

Today, her focus is primarily the Regency and Civil War eras, although Anna enjoys almost any period in American and British history. She would love to connect with any of her readers on her website – www.annastclaire.com, through email – annastclaire author@gmail.com, Instagram – annastclaire_author, BookBub – www.bookbub.com/profile/anna-st-claire, Twitter – @1AnnaSt Claire, Facebook – facebook.com/authorannastclaire or on Amazon – amazon.com/Anna-St-Claire/e/B078WMRHHF.

9 781956 003857